Deadly Embrace

Also by Trudy Labovitz

Ordinary Justice

Deadly Embrace

Trudy Labovitz

Spinsters Ink
Duluth, Minnesota
USA

First edition published October 2000
10-9-8-7-6-5-4-3-2-1

Spinsters Ink
32 E. First St., #330
Duluth, MN 55802-2002
USA

Cover design by Sarin Design
Cover art by Celeste Gallup Laub. Misty Mountain © 2000

Production:

Camila Aguilar	Tracy Gilsvik
Liz Brissett	Marian Hunstiger
Charlene Brown	Claire Kirch
Prudy Cameron	Joan Oswald
Helen Dooley	Kim Riordan
Joan Drury	Nancy Walker

Library of Congress Cataloging-in-Publication Data

Labovitz, Trudy, 1954-
   Deadly embrace/Trudy Labovitz.--1st ed.
      p. cm.
   ISBN 1-883523-38-9 (alk. paper)
   1. Women private investigators--West Virginia--Fiction. 2. West Virginia--Fiction. I
Title.

PS3562.A2355 D43 2000
813'.54--dc21   00-030114

Acknowledgements

Thanks are due many people who helped me see this book to completion. I couldn't have done it without the advice and support of my mother, Pearl Labovitz, friends extraordinaire Debbie Bailey, Celeste Laub, Celeste and Kelly McWhirter, Cele Bonomo, Kathy Emery, Jean Oertel, Carol Fryday and Dan Kamin, Marjorie and Bill Lewis, Laura Wholey, my sister Sherrie Labovitz, my other sister Barb Keacher, Carol and Allen Tulip, and the real Zoe, who kindly let me use her name.

Special thanks, also, to Celeste Gallup Laub, for painting another beauty of a cover.

My gratitude to everyone at Spinsters, especially Joan Drury.

And for those who spurred me on, allowed me to explore ideas and shed frustrated tears on their shoulders, thanks to the late, but not forgotten, Siegfried and Yoda Tierney, the most wonderful KJ, Aggie, and Katie, the steadfast Mr. Grey, and most of all, to Kaylo, Mischa, Dickens, Seeger, and you, too, Meadow.

For My Mom
For Everything

Prologue

Even when Ren clenched her eyes shut, she could still see the shooting play itself out—again and again. Who could she tell? Who would believe her?

Sounds of the party in the living room were as strong as ever. The bass made the walls vibrate. With all the laughter and tinkling of glass that filled Ren's ears, the gathering might just as well be taking place in her bedroom. She tried burrowing deeper into the pillow.

Ren's mother and the man she'd married must be having a good time. Ren could picture them smiling too much and throwing back their heads at what probably weren't even very witty remarks. They had no idea what had happened at Rosalyn's house just a few hours earlier.

Suddenly, Ren imagined throwing back the covers, jumping out of bed, and clomping downstairs the way her mother always told her not to. In her ratty flannel nightgown, dirty bare feet, and disheveled hair with its scarlet streak, she'd make a grand entrance. She could stand in the doorway, commanding everyone's attention, and announce what she had seen. Surely someone would believe her.

What an impression that would make on her mother's friends! Not that she particularly cared, but her mother's husband would hustle her to some private boarding school so fast, she'd never even be able to say good-bye to Billy Johns. It wouldn't matter if anyone at the party believed her or not.

Restlessly, Ren shifted her head, looking for a spot on her pillow untouched by tears.

No matter what she tried to think about, it couldn't erase the fact that two people had been shot. Almost in front of her face. She had to tell someone what she'd seen.

But who would believe her? She'd told so many lies, no one paid her much attention anymore, no matter what she said.

"What were you doing over there?" her mother would ask.

As long as she was committed to telling the truth, Ren would have to answer, "I was smoking dope in my little hideout under the tree."

That should go over well. Ren sniffled. Why hadn't her mother noticed something was wrong? Ren never watched the news. Never! When her mother came to check on her in the middle of the party, why hadn't she noticed that Ren was sitting bent toward the TV? Why hadn't her mother asked, "Ren, what's the matter?"

Then Ren could have spilled it all. And gratefully. But her mother never even noticed what Ren was watching. She fiddled with an earring and inquired, "Is your homework finished, Renata?"

At Ren's bleak nod, her mother had simply said, "Well, it's late, and it's a school night. I think it's time you got yourself off to bed."

Who would believe her about seeing the shooting, if not her own mother?

No, scratch that. It was another lie. Ren hadn't actually *witnessed* the sheriff and the deputy getting shot. From her hiding place under the blue spruce, she couldn't possibly have seen what happened at the end of the driveway across the creek. Her imagination went on, regardless, supplying her with the pictures of how it must have been.

Angrily, Ren turned on her side, moving her head from the new wet spot on the pillow. She was lying again. And wasn't that how she always got into trouble?

Still, she did know things that no one else knew. That much was the truth.

What she'd actually seen first was the sheriff's car driving past. She'd been smoking in her spot under the big blue spruce, had just happened to lift her head, and for a brief, panicked instant, thought she was going to be busted.

Then she'd relaxed. Sheriff Ethan McKenna didn't know the way across the creek. Besides, he would have gone to her house first and talked to her mother. That's what cops usually did.

In an easier frame of mind, Ren had assumed Rosalyn must also be in the car, simply because the road led right to her house. Rosalyn was a cop, too. Ren had seen her in the gray uniform, either going off to work or coming home.

Despite the woman's profession, Ren liked Rosalyn, mostly from what she had learned while spying on her from across the creek, crouching under her tree. She tried to keep an eye on Rosalyn's movements, interested in the yearningly romantic way that Rosalyn and her husband, Kirk, acted with each other. They were always touching or kissing or, once, Ren had seen them dancing close in the moonlight, hands on each other's faces.

Now, if the TV news was right, Rosalyn was dead. Maybe the

sheriff was, too. Ren didn't know for sure.

She'd been startled by the noise, just a few minutes after the Blazer had gone up the road. Gunshots—a lot of them in a very short amount of time—shattered the drowsy, drizzly quiet of the afternoon like fireworks.

Shortly after that, the two men had run down the front lawn of Rosalyn's house. The one who carried the gun barreled so fast across the slope of the hill that he ran out from under the knitted blue cap he wore. It plummeted to the grass like a wounded bird. The man hadn't even noticed.

It was the other one she recognized, the one without the gun. The two men were arguing, waving their arms around. At first, Ren had thought the one she knew was pointing toward her under the tree, and she quickly ducked her head, but—as she raised it again—she realized he was gesturing toward the car. Ren hadn't even been aware of the car.

It was a blue Plymouth Neon, but the driver's door was a different shade. It was parallel to the creek, in the small public parking area where locals pulled over to fish.

Still raising voices that rain damped by the time sound carried across the creek, the argument continued for a few seconds. Ren watched as the man who'd lost the hat glanced around the front yard. Once again, she lowered her head, although she was pretty sure no one could see her, even from her side of the creek. There was no sense taking chances when the guy had that gun.

When she looked again, the man with the gun was standing at the edge of the creek, still talking in an angry voice to the other man, who hadn't moved from the side of the car. He made a motion, as if intending to throw the weapon in the water, but abruptly changed his mind. Holding up a hand toward his companion, who suddenly fell silent, the man walked across the yard to a wooden structure. In a few seconds, the gun was gone. And so was a handful of what looked like pebbles that the man had removed from a jacket pocket. Afterward, brushing his hands together as if ridding them of dirt, he joined his cohort at the car.

Seemingly satisfied, the two men slid into their seats and slammed the doors. The man who'd thrown away the gun started the car with a roar so loud it made Ren jump.

When she had finished rubbing her head where she'd hit it against a lower branch, the car was gone. The joint burned her fingers as Ren took a final toke and filled her lungs with sweet smoke. What was she going to do now?

Ren rolled over, almost choking as her nightgown twisted under her. Maybe if she told Billy Johns, he wouldn't think she was lying. No, too big a risk. If she did tell him, and he didn't believe her, that would be the end. He wouldn't be her friend anymore.

And Ren didn't have any other friends.

Sometimes, she wasn't exactly sure Billy was her friend. He was always nice to her, and he usually smiled at her when he saw her. If he didn't hang out with her, that was okay. Billy was the star quarterback for the school. He was bound to have to divide his attention among a lot of people. Still, she didn't want to lose the little time she did have with him. It meant too much to her.

Maybe she should call the police. Ren slid her arm out from under the covers and reached for the phone by the bed, but she couldn't complete the movement. The trouble was—they knew her. She'd told them stories before. Some of them *were* lies, but not all of them. They hadn't believed her then; they wouldn't believe her now, either. And they'd want to talk to her mother. If her mother had to tell them again what a liar she was, this time Ren really would be sent away.

If they sent her away, she'd never see Billy Johns again.

Ren sniffled and ran a wet flannel cuff under her nose.

Maybe she could call the cops anonymously, just to report what she'd seen. But what if they had caller I.D.? They'd know who she was, and then they'd think she was lying.

The loud, grating laughter of the man who'd married her mother forced its way into Ren's room. How could her mother not see what a fake he was?

The sheriff had told her more than once that she could come to him with any problem. He knew who she was, had stopped and talked to her on a few occasions. Maybe he'd really meant it, although Ren had dismissed the idea at the time. But now, when she truly needed him, how could she test his sincerity, when he was one of the two who'd been shot?

Ren thought it was ironic laughter filling her, bubbling from her belly, right up until fresh, hot tears spilled over her cheeks like lava shooting up from the depths of the earth.

Willa Fiore parked herself down the hall from the Intensive Care Unit. The other reporters were segregated in the open waiting area on the main floor, but Russell Creek, West Virginia, was Willa's home turf, and if she couldn't find a way downstairs without anyone official knowing, then she wasn't half the reporter she considered herself to be. Besides, the sheriff was her friend Zoe's cousin, and Zoe would want to hear what Willa had to say.

Willa pushed her borrowed chair against the wall but focused her gaze sideways, on the police officer guarding the door of the I.C.U. She did not want to take a chance on missing Zoe.

The tough part was going to be keeping her job with the *Russell Creek Bulletin* while remaining Zoe Kergulin's friend. In this case, there was no way she could be loyal to both.

Ever since Zoe's best friend had been killed in Washington, D.C., three years earlier, Zoe hadn't held the media in very high esteem. If Willa took advantage of their friendship, even though it gave her a leg up on every other reporter currently in town, it would be the last time Zoe would talk to her. Willa knew that as well as she knew her own birthday. On the other hand, if she had no story all her own to turn over to her editor, she might as well be out looking for another line of work. The problem was—there was nothing else she'd ever wanted to do.

Right now, what she wanted to do was pace, but Willa settled for wiggling her foot where it dangled from her neatly crossed leg. That movement did little to dissipate the energy flowing through her blood. She needed to be moving, to be gathering information, but she also needed to be sitting and waiting for Zoe.

It had been at least eight hours since Ethan McKenna had been moved to this unit. Willa had obeyed the hospital rules and turned off her cell phone, effectively cutting herself off from everything else that might be happening. Her nerves twitched, knowing she was missing opportunities for other stories. Even though she was so close to the Intensive Care Unit, she couldn't get the scoop on how Ethan was doing.

She did know he'd been critically injured. And she knew the bullets that did the damage had entered him from the back, high on the left side. At the briefing following surgery, before his family had clamped down on any information being given out, the doctor had used a diagram to show how one bullet had ricocheted off Ethan's skull, another had gone clean through his hand, and two, maybe three, others had duked it out with the bone and tissue in his left shoulder.

"How was he shot from behind when he was driving the car?" one of the television reporters had asked.

"We can't say yet," Ed West of the state police had answered. "We believe that all the shots came through the window on the passenger side of the vehicle or through the windshield. The shooter stood on a low hillside above the car, roughly parallel to the car's front fender. We'll know more when the autopsy on

Deputy Sheriff Fitzgerald is complete and when we've finished our examination of the crime scene. Also, when Sheriff McKenna wakes up, maybe he'll be able to tell us more."

"Then, how do you explain how the sheriff was shot from behind?" the reporter repeated. Cameras continued to roll.

Ed West glanced grimly at the doctor. He pressed his lips together. At last, he said, "As near as we can determine, the sheriff was facing Deputy Fitzgerald, his back to the windshield."

"As in kissing her?" another of the television reporters had asked coyly, a lift of the eyebrow accompanying his question.

"Look, folks," Ed West had raised his hands in appeasement or surrender, "I'm not going to speculate about what the sheriff was doing."

Willa had been sickened by the humor even as her heart rate increased at the inkling of a good story. Behind her, she heard someone whisper, "I'll bet that's the last time he kisses with his eyes closed!"

"Maybe they'll find part of his tongue in her mouth. Or hers in his," a companion had answered. Laughter from both had quickly followed. A quick glance was enough for Willa to size up the men. She scowled.

"Wasn't the dead woman married?" a print reporter had asked.

"So?" answered one of the wits behind Willa.

When the call had come in, Willa had been quick enough to follow the paramedics up the highway, sticking with them through the twisted, winding turns they took, many on two wheels, until they stopped abruptly on a pitted road by a two-story clapboard farmhouse.

The front porch was propped with posts leaning in from the yard, and the stairs were gone. Cinder blocks and boards served as

3

makeshift steps. Replacement windows, some still sporting their brand name on stickers, stared from the front of the house.

Willa only noticed those things on the way back to her car, though. When she first arrived, all of her attention was focused on the ambulance crew. Heavy equipment weighing them down, they ran as if they had no time to spare.

As the curve of the drive flattened out, Willa saw Ethan's car. It was an older, white Blazer, rust creeping up from underneath, "Sheriff" emblazoned in large, red letters on both sides.

Chickie Ondean, Ethan's one-time mentor and now his lieutenant, stood at the edge of the blacktop, his face pale, his lower lip chewed and chapped. Rain spattered through the sparse gray hairs on top of his head, but he was unaware of it. His shirtfront was sticky with drying blood.

"Is he alive?" Chickie had asked, again and again, of those officers around him. "I couldn't find a pulse."

A rise beside the drive afforded Willa a view of the Blazer. From there, she had stood and watched, dispassionately scrawling notes. Rain splattered the pages, but as long as the ink held, Willa hardly noticed the weather, even though she was fastidious about her appearance. Her only concession to the rain was to hunch over her notebook, shielding it with her body as she wrote.

A paramedic crawled in the driver's side. Another reached in from the passenger side, brushing aside shattered glass as she instructed, "Make sure you put that collar on him, Mel. We're not moving him until that collar is on." She stepped back from the open doorway to call out, "Where's the body board? We need it here now!"

As the paramedic had turned, Willa saw Ethan. He lay face up around Rosalyn Fitzgerald's knees and looked as if he had slipped down from her lap. His head lolled at a disturbing cant, blood covering his chest, his left arm, his face, as if he'd been dipped like a confection in a vat of chocolate.

4

The paramedic in the car recoiled as the sheriff's left shoulder, which he'd touched accidentally, gave way beneath his hand.

"Geez, Elly," he said. "His shoulder's mush."

"Is the collar on? Keep some pressure on that shoulder!"

"What about the other one? The woman?" someone asked.

"She's cold already," Elly replied. "Where the hell is that 'copter?"

It was thanks to Willa, who had phoned Zoe even before she'd dialed her editor, that Ethan had someone waiting for him when the helicopter arrived at the hospital.

When she'd gotten around to dialing Josh at the *Bulletin*, she had told him exactly what she'd seen, composing the story from her notes as she related what she'd learned.

It wasn't that the *Bulletin* had higher journalistic standards than other media. It was more likely that the paper was the only truly local source of news. Although it was called the *Russell Creek Bulletin*, after the county seat, in fact it covered all of Bickle County, and it was the only media outlet that did. Therefore, Willa reasoned, it was more likely to downplay the talk of an affair between Ethan McKenna and Rosalyn Fitzgerald than were other sources of news. Ethan always got the paper's editorial endorsement, although sometimes it disagreed with his approach to problems.

On the whole, the paper realized just how lucky Bickle County was to have a sheriff who not only was clean but also worked hard to keep the entire department that way.

Accusations of the sheriff having an affair with one of his deputies would not sit well with county residents. Willa hoped she wouldn't be the one writing those stories.

The other papers would tell the tale readily enough. So would radio and television. As far as Willa knew, the stories were probably already spreading like the smell of fertilizer in a strong wind.

5

Standing, stretching the kinks out of her back, she walked several paces down the corridor toward the Intensive Care Unit.

The watch had changed. Another young officer had taken up the post just outside the double doors. This one wore a different uniform, but there was no mistaking the stance and the clipboard.

Earlier, Willa had attempted to brash her way in, asking the man on duty to check with Zoe to see if she shouldn't be allowed access.

"Sorry, ma'am," the young uniform had replied. "No one goes through those doors but families of patients, official investigators, and medical personnel. No exceptions."

Willa nodded to herself, made an abrupt about-face, and marched back to her own post. Surely soon, she thought, Zoe would relinquish her vigil and come down the hall.

Sleep wasn't coming easily for Ren Bertram. She kept imagining the shooting, her mind more than ready to show her what her eye had not actually seen.

According to what Ren had heard on the eleven o'clock news, Sheriff Ethan McKenna and Deputy Sheriff Rosalyn Fitzgerald had been having an affair right under the nose of Rosalyn's husband, Kirk. Who knew how long they'd been doing it?

The reporter said that Kirk Fitzgerald was being sought by police and the FBI. The FBI had been called in because this shooting was similar to those of three other law enforcement officials in recent months in other parts of the country.

It was kind of cool that the FBI was in town. Maybe, Ren thought, she should call them and make her usual report. Maybe they would believe her.

Did police in Bickle County share what they knew with FBI agents? If they did, and if she called and her name popped up on the FBI computer screen, then right under her name it would say,

"Liar. Says anything and everything. Don't believe a word of it."

Maybe she could just go to Rosalyn's house and knock on the door and ask for the FBI. Maybe she could make a report without saying who she was.

Ren started laughing then, tears leaking out of her eyes again and soaking into her pillowcase, as she pictured herself—high, most likely—and sporting that telltale streak of red hair, trying to remain anonymous.

Then she thought of Rosalyn Fitzgerald, who was dead now. Rosalyn had sure put on a good show of loving her husband. Maybe she was just a good actor. Maybe she'd known Ren was watching from under the blue spruce, trying to learn what it meant to love someone. To be loved.

Rosalyn wouldn't ever kiss anyone again. She'd never dance across the yard in her husband's arms. There would probably not ever come another time in Ren's life when she could spy on two people sharing an apple, juice running down their chins and their T-shirts, their lips kind of teasing each other.

Ren sighed and flopped to her side, further twisting the covers underneath her. Her favorite nightgown kept trying to choke her. The party had been over for hours. Her mother and that man she'd married had gone to sleep hours earlier. The sky was already beginning to brighten. No matter how much she turned it over, Ren still couldn't think of a single person she could tell about what she had seen at Rosalyn's house.

Grit the size of popcorn propped open Zoe's eyes as she slumped in the vinyl-covered chair near Ethan's bed. Never before had she thought of her cousin as small or shrunken. Always, he had been like an older brother: taller, protective, sometimes even looming. Now, the banks of machines and their tubular appendages dwarfed him, swallowed him up. Zoe had to stand beside the bed just to see him.

There was a rhythm to the heart monitor, the blood oxygen monitor, the ventilator, but none was in sync with the others.

A line had been carved between Ethan's eyes, as if he still managed to feel pain, however deep the coma. And his mouth, which was always so quick to smile, now turned down in a frown that reflected nothing of the Ethan she knew.

Zoe sipped from the cup of cold coffee that had become attached to her hand at some time earlier. She made a face at the taste but swallowed anyway.

She had just spent endless minutes in a small space that aspired to be a room. Apparently, doctors conferred or wrote notes there. In actuality, Zoe hadn't paid much attention to whatever it might be used for. All she knew was that it was close to Ethan, but not close enough for her to see him.

The authorities had assured her someone was with him while they questioned her, but there had been no one watching guard over him when she had been permitted to return. What if whoever had shot him the first time came back for a second try?

Not that her body would stop someone from putting yet another bullet into her cousin, but at least she could attempt to prevent it.

Despite her best intentions never to carry a gun again, she desperately wanted to dash over to Ethan's house, open one of the locked boxes he kept there, and grab all the firepower she could find. The only thing that prevented her from charging out of the hospital was the fact that she'd have to leave Ethan unprotected while she ran the errand. She would not leave his side.

A body pitched itself into the chair beside hers. Zoe straightened to find herself staring at a hand outstretched toward her. The man attached to the appendage looked almost as spent as she did. She figured he must be federal or state law enforcement, since he had managed to get by the guard, but he had not been among those who had questioned her. Her glance bounced between the man's hand and his face.

"Andrew Prescott," he introduced himself. "Hold on. I have some I.D. here somewhere."

As he hauled himself up to search his jeans pockets, Zoe saw a tall man, on the thin side, hair blond and perhaps an inch or two too short, face pale where a razor had recently had contact, and eyes a remarkable shade of gray, flecked with green or blue.

"Geez, I do this all the time," he told her. "You'd think I'd remember which pocket I put it in. Wait, I know I have it."

"What kind of I.D. are you looking for?" Zoe asked with a tired smile.

"I'm a state cop." With a triumphant exclamation, Andrew Prescott produced a small leather folder and flipped it open for Zoe's examination. "Don't you find it impressive when people can just pull them out and flash them? Then there's me. I never learned the cool flip in training."

"Drug Enforcement," Zoe observed. "What's a narc doing here?"

As he folded the I.D. away in his jeans pocket and patted it sheepishly, as if to remember, Andrew slipped back into the chair beside Zoe.

"We're working on a sting just next door in Feller County." He ran a hand across the smooth skin of his chin. "Well, we were. Sometimes we'd cross the line into Bickle County unavoidably. I've been working with Sheriff McKenna on and off for some time now, but Feller County has been the main area of concentration."

He stopped his explanation and glanced toward Ethan, his expression unreadable. "I was really sorry to hear about what happened to Ethan and that deputy. It's a terrible thing. He's your cousin, isn't he?"

"Yes."

"He's a good guy. Not only straightforward, but on the level. He knows this county inside and out, and I think he'd do anything to protect the people here. Most sheriffs and police chiefs I've met are more interested in protecting their own jobs, their own behinds, and their own bad elements than the people they're actually *supposed* to protect. Not Ethan McKenna."

It wasn't that Zoe hadn't heard the same from others, but in the Intensive Care Unit, with Ethan maybe slipping away, the words sounded too much like an epitaph. Unable to trust her voice, she merely nodded.

Andrew went on in a lower tone of voice, "I'd met Rosalyn

Fitzgerald once or twice. Ethan was grooming her for bigger things. She seemed to have a lot of potential."

"That's what I've heard," Zoe said, ignoring the break in her voice.

Andrew Prescott studied her a moment before saying, "I hear you used to work for the Department of Justice."

"A long time ago." It had been three years since she had resigned, three years since her friend Karen had been murdered.

Nodding knowingly, Andrew shrewdly inquired, "Did you get into the work because of him?" He cocked his head toward Ethan.

"What makes you ask that?" It was the truth, but Zoe wasn't about to confide it to a stranger.

A crooked smile crept across Andrew's lips and quickly darted away. He shrugged. "I was thinking of my brother. Drugs killed him when I was only twelve. From that moment on, I knew I was going to wear a white hat and fight the bad guys.

"Ethan told me he'd wanted to be sheriff ever since he'd seen his aunt—your mother, I assume—get beaten by the sheriff's deputies while she peacefully walked a picket line at a coal mine. Most people, seeing that, they'd want to grow up and beat up the damn deputies. Ethan, he wanted to get rid of all the corruption and do the job right."

Zoe followed Andrew's gaze to where Ethan lay. The sounds of machines and monitors once more filled the small space.

"You know, I really wish we had this sting going in Bickle County. Do you know Sheriff Shep Tuttle?"

Zoe had heard of the Feller County sheriff, and she knew that he had a reputation as a politician and a blowhard, although she had heard nothing about him from Ethan's lips.

"Not really," she replied.

"Well, you're lucky. The guy's an idiot and a buffoon. He can't reason, can't see the good of anything that doesn't benefit him personally. He's dyslexic and won't admit to it—or to making any mistake—and he wants his fingers in every pie."

Andrew slipped lower in the chair, unfolding his long legs out in front of him. He sighed. "I'm sorry. I shouldn't be bad-mouthing a cop. It's just that after this shooting, my whole operation is suspended. I've spent almost two years setting myself up around the state as a drug dealer. I was just about to meet a local contact that we'd worked hard to get. Harder and longer than I've worked with any other county in the program, if you want to know the truth. Finally, everything was falling into place. And then it gets called off.

"Not that I mind saying good-bye to the filth for a while. Geez, last night was the first good shave I've had in months. Not to mention the luxury of a bath. A haircut, too. And clean clothes. People just saw the long hair and the beard. I limped a bit, too, just to change my walk. No one should recognize me now."

A smile softened the lines of his face, lighting him up from within. "I lost my place in my rant some time ago, didn't I? Lack of sleep, I guess. Ah, well, I guess my point was that if my bosses had let us set the sting up with Bickle County's cooperation instead of Feller's, this case would have been wrapped up a while ago. Ethan would have done his best to throw the resources of the county behind us. We'd know all the dealers and every one of their suppliers. All Sheriff Tuttle wanted to do was throw obstacles in front of us.

"For some reason, he's got the political clout to swing it that way. He told me Ethan was always getting the glory, and he wanted some, too. Now the operation's on hold, at best. Two years setting the thing up, two damn years of not only my career but my life, too, and then I get pulled off because of the heat of this shooting."

He clamped a hand over his mouth. "I just heard how terrible and unfeeling that sounded. I apologize. I didn't mean that by getting shot, Ethan and Rosalyn screwed up my bust. That was unforgivable of me."

Zoe shrugged empathetically. "You invested a lot of time, a lot of energy. You look as if you haven't slept for a while. Who wouldn't be upset, given those circumstances?"

"I'm an idiot. As big an idiot as Shep Tuttle. Look, I really stopped by to see if there was anything I could do for you. Can I get you some coffee? Run any errands?"

"Nothing, thanks," Zoe said, shaking her head, although she knew there were hundreds of things that had to be done. For the moment, though, all of them could wait.

They sat silently for a few minutes, listening to the steady repetition of the machines. Zoe watched the drip of the I.V. Her eyes felt grittier with each blink, and the skin over her cheekbones seemed stretched taut enough to crack.

It was Andrew who broke the silence. "You ever lose someone you loved?"

She recoiled at the question but immediately saw the tears glistening in his eyes.

"You thinking of your brother?" she asked quietly.

He nodded and used the back of one hand to wipe his eyes. "Geez, I'm more tired than I thought. I thought all that hurt had healed. Just being here, in a hospital, makes it all seem so recent, even though my brother died years ago."

"I think grief is like a minefield," Zoe said, having had years herself to think about the concept. "The hurt never does heal or go away. You just come to learn that there are safe places to step where your grief won't blow up on you. In the beginning, you walk slowly, testing each footfall. As time goes on, you learn the way and can neatly sidestep when necessary. But sometimes, unavoidably, your foot leaves the trodden path for just a moment, and boom!"

She raised her hands and separated them, simulating a mushroom cloud.

Andrew blinked rapidly, nodding. "That could be it."

He straightened. "So, how come you left Justice? I heard you were a real go-getter. Someone told me you helped implement the first consent decree between Justice and a police department. That must have been gratifying. Promotion-rocket-ship to the top, huh? They must have hated losing you."

Zoe smiled ruefully, feeling the skin rasp across her face. "I was a go-getter all right, but I didn't always go in the direction I was supposed to. I followed the evidence, wherever it took me. You step on toes, you don't exactly ride the rocket ship to the top. Still, I enjoyed the job. Very much. It had an impact."

"So why did you leave?" he repeated.

She shrugged. "It was time to move on."

"I can't believe anyone would leave that kind of work voluntarily. I love going after the bad guys."

Shrugging again, Zoe said, "It's good to do something your heart's in."

He shook his head. "It might be better to do something your mind's in. No, that's not quite it. Let's say I have a tendency to speak before my mind even comes into the picture. I've offended a few people myself by keeping my eyes on the case and paying no attention to politics. That's how I ended up assigned to a sting in Feller County. And I think I was doubly cursed by having to work so closely with Sheriff Tuttle. It was like payback for all the kowtowing I didn't do when I had the chance. I was zipping through this assignment, not even really minding the filth, and then I hit the Feller County roadblock: Shep Tuttle." Andrew looked frustrated.

"Still," Zoe observed, "you have an opportunity to make an impact."

"Yeah. Maybe I still will. Meanwhile, the thing's in limbo. I don't want to go back without another bust. Otherwise, I've wasted too much time. Of my job *and* my life. Once things on the street have cooled down a bit, maybe I can get this thing back on track."

Zoe nodded, yawning hugely.

"Hey," Andrew said. "How about we get some breakfast? What is it, eight or nine already? The coffee shop should be open."

"No, thanks," Zoe said. She was staying put until someone showed up to take over her vigil. Some of her bothers and sisters were already on their way. And Ethan's brother, Eric, had immediately volunteered to hire a private security firm to provide protection for his brother. Eric was a lawyer, wealthier no doubt, than most of her siblings combined, and Zoe had heartily seconded the proposal when it had been offered. Until it was clear who had attempted to kill Ethan, Zoe and Eric agreed that trained outside personnel were less likely to be involved in the crime than anyone local. If state or county police wanted to keep a presence at the door to the I.C.U., all the better.

The hospital staff already knew that Zoe was determined to stay, whatever the regulations of the I.C.U. They would adjust to a security presence as well.

Soon, either the private cops or someone from her own family would arrive; then Zoe would begin asking her own questions about who had shot her cousin and Rosalyn Fitzgerald. Until then, however, she would not be moved.

Willa felt her mouth pull down in a grimace. Trying to shake off the insistent hand on her arm, she jerked. Her mind presented her with the image of the nurse or orderly who had so confidently strolled down the corridor that her eye had been attracted to him. And when he caught sight of her catching sight of him, he'd smiled, run his tongue over his teeth with a sucking noise, and then said, "Oh, how I do love the taste of brown sugar."

What Willa had replied was unprintable in the *Bulletin*, and even most of the tabloids, whatever their standards.

In sleep, she smiled as she replayed the man's slow double take.

Then, the hand moved from her arm to her shoulder. "I told you once," she muttered, the words forming in her dream but surprising her into wakefulness when she heard their harsh echo off the corridor walls.

Willa's eyes opened in sudden, disoriented panic and found themselves locked into Zoe's. Zoe straightened, letting her hand fall away.

"I must have been sleeping," Willa muttered, rubbing at her eyes with the flat of her palms. Her back hurt, and the muscles in her shoulders ached. Something dry in the corner of her mouth pulled at her skin. Had she drooled in her sleep?

"How's Ethan?" she asked through a yawn, unable to stifle it.

With a face devoid of emotion, a face almost unrecognizable in its lack of expression, a face waxen in appearance and smudged darkly beneath the eyes, Zoe said, "He's coming along."

Her friend's appearance belied her words, but Willa merely nodded.

"Can you give me directions, Willa?" Zoe asked. "I don't know how to get to Rosalyn Fitzgerald's place."

"Zoe," Willa said, rising with a quick touch to her friend's forearm. She had suddenly remembered why it was so important she park herself where Zoe would be certain to find her.

As if crossing a busy street, Willa looked left, then right, and then left again. Satisfied that they were alone, she said, "Zoe, it wasn't you. You hear me? It wasn't someone out to get revenge on you."

For the first time, there was a distant spark of life in Zoe's eyes. "How do you know?"

Willa could see the dryness of Zoe's lips, how thin flakes of skin lifted like lizard scales into the air. A good lipstick, or even a moisturizer, would prevent that, but Zoe never thought about those things, Willa found herself reflecting irrelevantly. She shook the sleep from her head.

"While Ethan was in surgery, I did some checking. Also, I called your friend Beth at the FBI. You gave me her name to use as a source once, remember? Anyway, Paul Martin's brother and his friend—the one who made the threats right after Paul Martin's funeral—are both serving active duty in the National Guard. There was major flooding south of us, and they're both down there. I checked on that cop from eastern Pennsylvania, too. Well, that ex-cop."

"Neil Yeager," Zoe supplied, her eyes focused on Willa, her breathing shallow at best. Unable to put voice to it, she had not dared to imagine that association with her had something to do with the terrible consequences that had befallen her cousin and his deputy.

"Yeah, him. He was on a gambling junket to Atlantic City with a social group from his church. The pastor, who told me I pulled him away from a slot machine that was about to blow, backed up that alibi all the way. Your friend Beth is still checking other possibles, but Zoe, it doesn't look like this is in any way connected with you."

Zoe's jaw moved, as if trying to relieve stiffness, and it looked to her friend as if she took several deep breaths. "You're certain?"

"Hey babe, I'm a good reporter. You're not Typhoid Mary. Deal with it."

Briefly, Zoe gripped Willa's shoulder. The faint trace of a smile backlit her face without actually showing on her lips. She nodded. "Thank you."

"Just doing my job as a friend," Willa shrugged, as if the effort had truly been nothing, but she scowled to herself. Choosing between breakout stories and fledgling friendships wasn't one of the topics that had been covered in any of her journalism classes.

"Can you give me those directions?" Zoe asked, her voice low even though they were alone in the corridor.

"You're in no shape to drive. How about we both get some sleep and then we go?" Willa sighed when she saw the light leave Zoe's face as if fleeing. "Actually, I'm not sure I can give you directions. I wasn't paying attention to exit names and street signs. I was too busy trying to stay on the road and not lose sight of the cars in front of me. But I'm pretty sure I could find it. Come on. I assume you want to go now. Want me to drive?"

"That's it! Pumpkin Cave. Take that exit!" Willa pointed to the right, and Zoe swerved onto the ramp almost too late. Following Willa's finger, Zoe turned north after the stop sign at the end of the ramp. With a wrinkled forehead, Willa studied the roadside for landmarks she had only subliminally noted the last time she had driven this road.

"There should be a turnoff up ahead," Willa pronounced slowly. "Then we go over a bridge. Turn there. Maybe."

She saw the narrow bridge on the left. Recalling the ambulance taking at least one turn on two tires, Willa indicated where she thought Zoe should go.

"The next turn should be a left onto a dirt lane. Or maybe it's paved. I'm not sure. But from there, you'll be able to see Rosalyn Fitzgerald's house." Swiveling her head, Willa continued in some exasperation, "It's more overgrown here than I remember. Maybe I'm wrong. Wait, what's that?"

The lane did curve around the front of a farmhouse, but this one appeared to be abandoned. The front porch sagged toward the sparse lawn, but its roof was unsupported by timbers. What remained of the windows facing the road were probably the original six-over-sixes. Shards of glass, either knocked to the ground or still managing to cling to the frames, glittered.

Willa muttered to herself, then said out loud, "This is *almost* the right place."

With the same blank, unreadable expression, Zoe kept her hands on the wheel, waiting.

"We made a wrong turn somewhere. Has to be. This place, it's not what we're looking for. Let's head back toward the exit ramp. I know we were okay up to there."

Silently, Zoe retraced the route back to the highway exit. Once again, they headed north. Willa remembered the turn onto the narrow bridge, but as they approached the bridge for the second time, Willa said, "Just go straight here."

She was unsure she would recognize anything from that point on. Weariness was creeping into her thought processes and interrupting synapses. Her recollections might not be trustworthy.

Ahead, on the right, was another narrow bridge. Zoe slowed as Willa scanned the landscape. All Willa remembered was the speed of the ambulance and the police cars and the scream of the sirens. Nevertheless, she nodded to the right.

"Turn here, across that bridge."

Not far after the turn, a rusting tractor sitting by the roadside jogged something in Willa's memory. She leaned forward, searching.

"Go left here, onto this little road."

The water they had just crossed burbled over rocks and cut a deep channel beside the narrow lane. Trees bent over the bank, and errant brown leaves dashed back and forth across the weathered reeds like kittens chasing a feather.

For the life of her, Willa did not remember the stream. She opened her mouth to ask Zoe to turn around again when a familiar two-story farmhouse with makeshift frontporch came into view. Replacement windows faced the road, reflecting the gray-tinged clouds overhead. Yellow police tape stretched from the center porch post to a tree on the other side of the lane.

"This is it, Zoe. Come on, I'll show you where the Blazer was."

At first, Zoe did no more than stand near the end of the driveway in the spot where Ethan's car had been parked. The front lawn of the house sloped up toward the porch, which was sheltered by a line of seven or eight hemlocks. Bricks laid down in a basket-weave pattern cut steps and a path through the trees before curving across the lawn and up toward the porch.

Zoe shivered as a light rain began to fall, but she ignored it. Willa watched as her friend strode the twelve or fifteen feet up the steep hill until she was behind the trees. Her arm poked through the branches. Had she held a gun, she would have had a clear line of sight to the car while being completely hidden from view. In addition, she would have had the further advantage of shooting down from a height of several feet.

Two people trapped in the metal box of a car would have had a very tough time seeing where the shots were coming from, let alone pulling their own guns and returning fire.

Zoe's eyes traveled along the muddied ground. She knew the police would have been over the area thoroughly; if there were any evidence to be found, they would have found it. But that knowledge could not prevent her from parting the lower branches of the hemlocks and searching through the dirt with her fingers, hoping, Willa knew, to stumble onto a clue.

"Zoe," Willa said after a while, and not for the first or even the second time, "the police were all over this area. They didn't find anything, either." Her cell phone was in her hand, and she shoved it into her purse.

"No shells?" Zoe's fingers continued to sift through the earth.

Willa sighed, straightened, studied the dingy sky. "Zoe, there's something I have to tell you. I don't know how else to say it except straight out: the local and nearby media are sharing similar headlines in their next editions and newscasts. They go something along the lines of 'Local Sheriff Shot, Deputy Killed, in Love Nest.'"

Zoe reached farther under the hemlock, holding a branch out of the way of her face.

"I want you to know I didn't write the story or the headline. I just think you should know what's coming down."

Slowly, using the tree for leverage, Zoe pulled herself up. "It's not true. Ethan was not having an affair with Rosalyn Fitzgerald. He wouldn't."

"You know, he told me he was gay," Willa said. "Actually, I figured he had to be. I mean, he's so appealing, and yet he's still single. Heck, I don't know if he ever told you, but I asked him out once. He was so nice about turning me down. But Zoe, maybe he still has urges for a woman. It wouldn't be unheard of if he swung both ways."

With her thumb, Zoe crumbled dirt from her fingers. "Ethan has a favorite saying, Willa. Off the record now, right?" She waited for Willa's nod. "He tells every one of his deputies, 'Don't mess your nest.' Ethan wouldn't have sex with a subordinate. It wouldn't happen, Willa. Male or female, it wouldn't happen."

Grabbing both of Zoe's shoulders, Willa breathed hard. Zoe felt the hot exhalation on her cold skin.

"Come sit down here on the porch for a minute. I have something else to tell you."

Perplexed, Zoe nevertheless did as she was asked, ducking under the police tape and hoisting herself up backward to sit on the wooden floor of the porch, her feet dangling. Willa easily boosted herself up to sit beside her friend.

"While you were busy under those trees, I called to find out about the autopsy on Rosalyn Fitzgerald." The worst part about waiting for Zoe had been having so many questions unanswered and no way to ask them. In every hospital entrance had hung a huge sign telling visitors and staff to turn off cellular phones. So, Willa had sat in deliberate isolation for hours without being able to contact a single other person. While Zoe explored the shooting scene, Willa had taken the opportunity to get back in touch. "Have you heard anything?"

If possible, Zoe's expression became even more set. It was as if her features had petrified from wood to stone. She shook her head.

"Well, babe, the preliminary report is out. There are still tests to be run, but the medical examiner already knows a lot.

"Listen, Zoe, it's not that I enjoy hurting a friend, but you've got to know this. All of Ethan's wounds are from behind. If he'd simply been sitting at the wheel, the entry wounds would have been from the front—or at least the side. From the position of Rosalyn Fitzgerald's wounds, Ethan's wounds, and the bullet holes in the car, the police know the shooter was standing just about where you figured—where you were just looking for evidence—about thirteen feet away from the passenger-side front fender and above the car. If the shooter had moved, going around the car to shoot the other after hitting the first, either Ethan or Rosalyn would have had a chance to draw a weapon, but neither had the opportunity. Both of them were shot at exactly the same time.

"Do you understand what I'm saying, Zoe? The only way Ethan could have been shot in the back, given the position of the bullet holes in his car, is if he were facing Rosalyn, practically sitting in Rosalyn's lap."

Willa interrupted her argument in response to the slightest lifting of Zoe's chin. Rain, which had slackened, had begun to fall again, but Willa took no notice. She held up a hand like a traffic cop expecting full compliance.

"You're going to tell me Ethan was maybe talking to Rosalyn, that he was maybe leaning toward her before she got out of the car."

The only response from Zoe was the quickened cadence of her breathing. In Willa's mind appeared the image of a wild horse, nostrils flared, snorting in defiance.

Willa reached for Zoe's hand, but Zoe drew it away, disallowing the touch. Shrugging, Willa pointed to the ring on her own hand. She would not be stopped. "Zoe, Ethan wears some kind of a ring on his left hand. When the bullet went through his hand, it took a piece of that ring with it. Do you know where that piece of ring ended up? In Rosalyn Fitzgerald's teeth, through her right cheek. Now, you tell me, if it wasn't a caress, then what the hell was Ethan's hand doing on Rosalyn's face?"

Despite growing anger at herself for continuing to push when Zoe was already down, Willa found herself unable to stop. "And that's not all, Zoe. At least two bullets, and maybe more, passed through Ethan before entering Rosalyn Fitzgerald. Have you heard about all the blood they found on Rosalyn? It was Ethan's. Rosalyn died almost instantly, shot through the head and the chest, probably as Ethan slipped from her lap. She didn't bleed, not the way Ethan did.

"The bullets all went through him from the left side, entering through the back. And through her on the right, from the front. They were in each other's arms, Zoe. They had to be. That also accounts for why neither of them had a chance to draw a weapon. They just didn't see anyone outside the car. There's no other way to explain it."

After studying the unresponsive, clenched-teeth expression on the woman sitting beside her, Willa dropped her eyes. "I'm sorry."

Zoe pushed herself from the porch, landing heavily on her feet. Rain hit her head and shoulders.

"I have work to do," she said, dusting off her hands as she faced Willa. Then she turned and walked back across the yard, toward the end of the driveway where Ethan's Blazer had sat only the day before.

As she approached the hemlocks, she heard tires on gravel behind her. Spinning around, she ran back toward her friend, sudden panic fueling her.

"Get down, Willa!" she shouted, motioning with her arms. She vaulted onto the porch and practically tackled Willa to get her out of the line of sight.

In the parking area below the house, a white sedan braked to a stop. The noise of the engine abruptly ended. A door opened. As the cooling fan ticked under the hood, Zoe lifted her head from the rough lumber of the porch floor. She kept a warning hand on Willa's shoulder, letting her know she should stay where she was.

Had she been pressed, perhaps she wouldn't have been able to articulate the source of her panic. She knew Willa was wrong about Rosalyn Fitzgerald and Ethan. And if her friend was wrong about them, maybe she was wrong about someone who might still be gunning for a former employee of the Justice Department.

Standing beside the car, a perplexed expression on his face, stood Andrew Prescott, the state narcotics agent. Even from the distance across the lawn, Zoe could see the wrinkled line of his lips and the converging caterpillars of his eyebrows. Raindrops spattered his blue shirt.

"Zoe Kergulin!" he called out. "Are you okay?"

He walked to Zoe's old Chevy, looking in the windows, front seat and back. When he turned back toward the house, he saw Zoe standing on the porch, one hand extended to Willa, who was too busy brushing off her clothes to notice the proffered help.

A smile transformed Andrew Prescott's face as he bounded across the lawn toward the duo on the porch. "You ducked out of the hospital so fast, I didn't get a chance to give you the coffee I bought. And I had to drink it on the way out here, just to keep awake."

"You came all the way out here just to give me an empty cup of coffee?"

Glancing up from an unidentified spot on her jacket, Willa smiled. The voice she had heard sounded, for the first time that day, like her friend Zoe's.

"Sure, if you want it. But I came with a message from Libby Gordon, the FBI agent in charge of the investigation. She wants to make sure you keep out of it."

Zoe nodded. "Message received."

"And I came to tell you that the FBI has pretty much discarded the theory that the shooter might be anyone holding a grudge against you. Apparently, alibis check out."

"How did you know where to find me?"

"It was my first choice. This is where I would have wanted to go. One of the local deputies gave me directions."

"Wasn't Rosalyn Fitzgerald married?" Zoe asked suddenly, turning to Willa.

"Yes. His name is Kirk. No children."

"Where is he? Where was he yesterday?"

"I don't know. The police are trying to locate him, last I heard."

Zoe turned her eyes back to Andrew Prescott, silently throwing her question to him.

Still standing in the rain, he threw up his hands. "I thought you got the message about not butting into the investigation. You could be facing federal charges."

"So indict me. Where is he?"

"He works in Wheeling during the week, only comes home on weekends. From what I understand, the police found him in Wheeling yesterday. He's still being questioned." Andrew Prescott dropped his jaw, sighed, and looked toward his car before turning back. "Please, please don't ask me anything more. I want to help you, but you know you're too close to the investigation. You could ruin the government's case if you get involved."

Even as she did it, Zoe knew it was a mistake to rub her eyes. She looked at Andrew through slits that burned as if exposed to dozens of newly diced onions.

She suddenly jerked her head toward the parking area by the stream. "I just saw movement over there!"

Jumping from the porch, Zoe ran across the wet grass of the

27

front lawn. Oblivious to the rain and the chill on her skin, she dashed to the water's edge and peered through the gauzy curtain of storm to the other side of the stream.

A huge blue spruce stood lonely guard on the bank, its long branches sweeping the ground like tiered layers of a ball gown.

Zoe stared until her focus grew fuzzy. Andrew Prescott pulled up beside her with Willa right behind, holding the back of her jacket over her head, attempting to provide herself some scant protection.

"I don't see anything," Andrew pronounced at last. "Maybe it was a deer. Or a turkey or something."

Zoe stared, but the strength of her will alone was not enough to force whatever or whoever it had been to materialize in the meadow or the woods behind the spruce.

"Or something," Zoe echoed. "Maybe so."

Zoe awoke with a start, as if to a gunshot. Cherry Pie, the brown tabby curled beside her on the pillow, lifted his head and blinked, big-eyed.

She was in her own bed, fully dressed. She remembered intending to stretch out for no more than fifteen minutes the evening before. The cats needed her attention first, and then she was going to decide on something to feed her growing household of siblings and significant others.

Gray light filtered in through the magnificent hemlock outside her bedroom window, and Zoe squinted at the clock radio. It was six-thirty.

She yawned, cracking her jaw, and then jumped as the noise that had awakened her sounded again. Thunder, sharp and close.

Ethan had helped her patch the roof on her beloved Queen Anne, but she knew she was woefully behind in repair projects that should have been completed before winter set in, let alone before spring. Windows rattled in their frames, at least one piece of gutter had crashed and smashed, and mildew was traveling up the walls of the laundry porch like a mountain climber out to set new records.

None of it mattered.

Zoe picked up the phone and dialed the hospital. There was no change in her cousin's condition.

After a quick shower, she dressed and tiptoed downstairs.

Her niece, Piper, snored softly, curled fetally on the window seat at the landing. The usual vibrant colors of the stained glass window above her were oddly subdued, as if they, too, slumbered. A gray cat lifted her head from where it had been tucked against Piper's middle, soundlessly meowed, and jumped fluidly to the floor like water poured from a pitcher.

Zoe scooped up the little cat and buried her own nose in the soft fur as she continued down the stairs. Looking left, toward the front door, she saw a suitcase and a backpack. The pocket door to the front parlor was closed. Someone must have arrived since she had so precipitously crashed the night before.

Turning right, Zoe went down the hallway past the dining room on the left, the back parlor on the right, and veered into the kitchen, all the time rubbing a finger against the jawbone and cheek of the cat, Chocolate Pudding.

Red-eyed and pale, Zoe's sister Miriam sat at the old kitchen table, her chin in her palm. Her long hair was loose, not so much hanging down as floating in curly clouds around her head. With her right hand, she scrolled through an article on her laptop computer, muttering as she read. Beside her on the scarred wooden tabletop was an oily-looking cup of cold coffee. Miriam was a third-year resident in orthopedics, but she was quickly ingesting everything she could find on head trauma.

Zoe was surprised to see Andrew Prescott seated beside her sister. He slept, face down in his folded arms, a half-eaten piece of whole wheat toast crumbled under one elbow.

At the sink stood Zoe's nearest neighbor and newest friend, Kip Chaney. It wasn't the name she'd been born with, but it was the one she used now. Although their friendship had clicked immediately, Zoe figured she would never know Kip's original name. Asking was out of the question.

Zoe herself had picked up Kip from Philadelphia, where she'd arrived via Erie and Cleveland, from someplace farther west. Zoe knew that Kip had lived in hiding for three years before she'd ventured to attend a scientific conference in the limited field of particle physics that was her specialty.

Her estranged husband had been waiting for her there and had followed her to her hotel room. He had raped her, and in the process, broken her nose, her arm, and two ribs. She had barely escaped with her life.

Now, she lived at the farm up the mountain behind Zoe, supervising both the rehabilitation of the old house there and the day-to-day operation of the modern-day Underground Railroad that brought other abused women to and through Beverage, West Virginia.

Kip turned from the sink, quickly dried her hands, and hugged Zoe, who found herself blinking back unexpected tears.

In the doorway to the conservatory—the room devoted to cat trees and litter boxes—plainclothes detective Jennifer Randolph crouched and rubbed together her thumb and forefinger, trying to entice Hot Fudge, the newest and shyest of Zoe's four cats, into showing more of his beautiful, long-haired self.

"He won't come as long as you're looking at him," Zoe observed. "Try ignoring him."

"Males!" Jennifer smiled broadly as she stood, her knees creaking. "That's my problem with all of them. They won't come as long as I'm looking at them."

While Andrew made a show of yawning and stretching, Zoe and Miriam greeted each other. Miriam gestured toward the computer screen.

"My roomie just sent me this from a British medical journal. It's about closed head injuries. It's fascinating, Zoe." Miriam pressed her lips together before going on. "You know, there's a good chance Ethan'll have some complications from this."

Zoe nodded, but it was clear that although she heard her sister's words, she did not believe them. What might be true of others was one thing. Ethan was another. "Whatever happens, we'll deal with it. Are we sure there's a security guard with him now?"

"No question," Jennifer Randolph supplied. "They let in your brother David, who's there now, but I got turned away."

"Zoe," Miriam tried again, resting her hand on her sister's arm, "they have Ethan on Dilantin already, in an attempt to try to control and possibly stave off seizures. He may not be able to do his job anymore. All these scans can only tell us so much—"

"Is he going to live?" Andrew asked. He was wide awake, although his face was pale and blotchy with the need for a shave.

"Well, his vital signs aren't quite stable yet," Miriam said. "He's getting respiratory support. And that shoulder is causing some concern. His condition is critical. But he's getting the best care he possibly can. I think he's got a good chance." Miriam smiled slightly, her lips curling toward her teeth, Zoe noticed, just the way they'd done when she was a baby.

Zoe slipped her arm back around Miriam's shoulders and quickly hugged her.

As she bent to pick up the empty cat food dishes, Zoe asked, "Jennifer, do you have any idea when Rosalyn Fitzgerald's body will be released to her family? Has a funeral been scheduled yet?"

Jennifer nodded, yawning. "What's today? Thursday? The funeral's been scheduled for Tuesday. The body's supposed to be released later today."

Cold drops of water dripped onto Zoe's arm as she entered the conservatory. Frowning up at the huge circle of arced windows, as if a stern warning would be enough to seal any leaks, Zoe shook her head. All of the windows needed to be recaulked. It wouldn't surprise her if they needed to be reseated, too. Rain puddled in two other places on the old flagstone floor.

Zoe blinked slowly. Despite the wet, chilly day, windows above and around the room caught the available light and tossed it onto the back wall, which obligingly glowed in chestnut hues.

"He'll be okay," she warmly greeted Hot Fudge as he wound around her ankles. He led her to more empty dishes, which had been generously scattered around.

There were litter boxes to be scooped before Zoe returned to the kitchen with the empty dishes. The scene there hadn't changed much, except that her brother Chad had appeared, yawning vigorously and scratching at the stubble on his chin. He gave Zoe a quick hug, then turned to the coffeepot as if pulled irresistibly to magnetic north.

Thrusting his chair back from the table, Andrew gained his feet in one lithe wave of motion. "I'm going to go check outside," he said. "A little exercise will get the muscles going. Anything I can do for you?"

Zoe shook her head and turned on the water in the sink. Footsteps faded down the hallway, and there was barely a sound as the front door closed with a light touch. No one still sleeping was likely to have been disturbed.

Jennifer said, "I hope you don't mind that he rode out here with me. He hangs around the station like a fifth wheel. I don't think the FBI is involving him much in their investigation. He worked mostly out of Feller County, but he doesn't want to hang out over there. It's kind of nice having him around. He's pleasant enough, and he's not bad to look at, either."

"It's okay."

"I came out to tell you that if there's anything any of us can do for you, we're all available." She half-shrugged. "That's not just me speaking. Everyone wanted you to know."

Zoe nodded without answering. Slowly she turned from the sink. With soap dripping down her arms like a sanitized surgeon, she thoughtfully leaned against the sink. "Did you know Rosalyn Fitzgerald well, Jennifer?"

"How do I answer that?" Jennifer accepted a cup of coffee from Kip, who poured one for herself before reaching into the freezer for a few ice cubes, as if she had long been an at-ease friend. Adding milk to her own mug, Jennifer shrugged and sighed as she slid her legs under the table. "I'm not sure anyone knew her really well. A while back, I tried to organize the women in the department. It wasn't a union or anything, not even a group with a title, but I thought it would be helpful if the women got together and discussed situations peculiar to us. You know, despite Ethan's best efforts, there are still some real sexist guys on the force. And sometimes people on all sides don't treat us seriously. Anyway, I ran the idea past Ethan first, and he saw no problems with it.

"That's another thing—" Jennifer stopped herself before she started down her tangent. She grinned and hit her head with the palm of her hand. "Too many thoughts at once. I'll get back to that in a minute.

"So, I talked to all of the women—all of the women in uniform, that is. Everyone except civilian help. They all showed up at our first meeting, except Rosalyn. She told me she never wanted to be associated with a side group of any kind. A cop was what she was, and that's how she wanted to be identified. She claimed she never ran into any problems she couldn't handle."

"Some people are pretty independent," Miriam pointed out,

punctuating her statement with a quick glance at her sister. Zoe was busy placing the last cat food dish in the drainer, and the significance of the remark went unnoticed. She dried her hands on her jeans, whisked away the cold mug of coffee in front of Miriam, and poured a fresh one.

Kip took Zoe's place at the sink, adding a couple of dishes from the table to the mug her friend had just put in the soapy water. Once more, she took up the dishcloth.

"We're cops, though," Jennifer said. "We stick together more than most."

A bakery box sat on the counter, tied in string. Someone had brought goodies. Zoe wrestled off the string and set down the opened box on the table, nudging it toward the middle.

"The way it seemed to me," Jennifer said, reaching for a chocolate-covered mound in the middle of the box, "is that she had trouble sharing the glory. She wanted all the responsibility, too. That's not what makes a good cop.

"Still, from what I saw, she was more than competent. Which brings me to the point I wanted to make before. All this talk about Ethan and Rosalyn having an affair. I heard the same blather when I got promoted. In fact, I heard it *each time* I got promoted. Especially when I went into plainclothes. Everyone said I must be sleeping with Ethan. Like geez, how else would a woman get promoted? You'd think not one of us has the brains or the initiative, the way some guys talk. And the worst part is—it's not only the guys.

"Anyway, I just wanted you to know—just because people say it—it doesn't mean it's true. Ethan would never mess his nest. I wouldn't, either. People get their noses out of joint when someone else gets the assignment or promotion they wanted. Even me. But that's life, folks."

After a pause she added, "And besides, even if they were kissing, it doesn't mean there was a full-blown affair."

At the pantry door, where she was picking out cat food cans, Zoe's jaw dropped in consternation. "Jennifer, did Ethan ever kiss you? Did he?"

"Well, hell, Zoe, I'm like four inches taller than he is."

Dispiritedly, Zoe filled cat food dishes. She was in no mood to argue with Jennifer; she had no energy for it. Waiting until her initial anger had passed, she asked, "Was anyone close to Rosalyn?"

Jennifer thought for a moment, one hand idly tracing a scar in the tabletop. With her tongue, she swiped at a piece of chocolate on her lip. "Not that I can think of."

"Isn't that strange?"

Jennifer shook her head, as if at a loss. "We have our loners, just like everyone else. If she wasn't stable, she never would have been kept on, let alone promoted. Hell, Zoe, you've got to know there's talk about you, too. You're a single woman living isolated in a big house. It doesn't mean there's anything untoward going on." She paused, smiled. "Well, not necessarily."

At the sink, Kip rolled her eyes toward Zoe with a sympathetic smile.

"What about her husband?" Zoe placed the cat dishes on the floor, petting Hot Fudge and Chocolate Pudding to encourage them to eat.

"I never heard her mention him. He spent the week out of town. I met him a couple of times at picnics and Christmas parties. Seemed nice enough, I guess."

"Does his alibi hold water?"

"I don't know. I'm not really privy to what's going on in the investigation. The county police haven't been asked to take part." Jennifer bit off a big chunk of the pastry and chewed vigorously.

Pulling out a chair, Zoe tucked herself in close to Miriam.

Touching a shoulder to her sister's, Zoe felt the same pressure in response.

As she recaptured Jennifer's eye, she asked, "Who do you think did the shooting?"

Jennifer scooped filling into her mouth and tilted her head, blatant in her bafflement. "I suppose my first guess would be the husband. Or, failing that, maybe a boyfriend, assuming Rosalyn was seeing someone on the side. I don't have any ideas after that."

"What about someone who might have been after Ethan?" Miriam chimed in, raising her eyes from the computer.

"They wouldn't have known he was going to be driving Rosalyn home," Zoe said. "From what I've been told, Rosalyn Fitzgerald had been getting rides from various people while her car was in the shop. Tuesday morning, she asked Ethan to drive her home that afternoon. I know Ethan does that. He's told me there's so little time to see everyone, giving them a ride home when they need one is a way to rectify that.

"So, if she only asked him that morning, no one else would have expected him to show up. It had to be someone who was out to get Rosalyn. Ethan ended up in the cross fire by accident, not design."

Zoe studied the tabletop and sighed. "Unless," she added.

Jennifer nodded, taking another bite of her pastry.

"Unless what?" Miriam demanded.

"Unless," Jennifer said, squaring her shoulders and dropping the remainder of the doughnut onto the table, "someone from the department, maybe some jealous-someone with a grudge against either one of them, heard about the arrangement to drive Rosalyn home, and rushed out there, knowing how isolated the place is. Then, all he or she would have had to do was wait for the sheriff's car to pull up at the house." Grimly, she made a gun out of thumb and first two fingers. "I guess we all know why the sheriff's department isn't involved in this investigation, huh?"

The front doorbell buzzed loudly, and Zoe winced, glancing at the kitchen clock. It was barely eight. Her siblings and other assorted relatives were sleeping, or trying to, after a long night.

As she hurried down the hall, trying to preclude a second summons, Zoe snatched a quick look toward the still form bundled under blankets on the window seat at the landing. Her niece slept on. Behind the closed door of the front parlor, stirrings could be heard. Nevertheless, she gingerly opened the front door, closed it behind her, and crept through the foyer to the outside door, easing its oiled hinges.

Andrew Prescott stood in front of the beveled glass, a hangdog expression on his face. An arm belonging to someone else was draped around his shoulders, but until she fully pushed open the door, Zoe was unable to tell who else was out there.

For an instant, panic seized her as she thought Andrew might be a hostage, but there was no fear in the man's eyes, only long suffering.

"I'm sorry, Zoe," Andrew said as soon as she opened the door. "I tried to tell him it was early, but law enforcement knows no time of day."

A man twice Andrew's bulk removed his hat and nodded. "Hello, Miss Zoe. I'm Sheriff Shep Tuttle. I do know it's early, and I do apologize if I woke you, but I want you to know if there's anything the Feller County sheriff and his department can do to make things easier for you, just let me know. Ethan McKenna's a good man, and he's a friend of mine. We'll be glad to help out in any way we can."

"Come in, Sheriff," Zoe said, stepping back. "I'm Zoe Kergulin. Just let me close this door before we open the inner one. I don't want to let the cats out."

"Cats? You one of those people who have cats? I don't see any cats."

"They're either eating or hiding," Zoe said as she locked the front door behind them. "There are a few more people here than they're used to."

"You've got a heck of a lot of cars blocking that road out there, Miss Zoe."

"Please," she said, ushering the two men down the central hall toward the kitchen. "Call me Zoe or call me Ms. Kergulin. I'd appreciate it, Sheriff. Either one is fine. And that's not a road. It's my driveway."

"Mighty long driveway."

"Yes, it is."

"Hello, folks," Shep Tuttle waved at the kitchen. "I'm Sheriff Tuttle, Feller County. Head on in there, Mr. Prescott. Have a seat. Have you met Mr. Prescott? He's with the state police. Used to be a long-haired, dirty son of a gun, but he's okay now, aren't you, Mr. Prescott?"

Resignedly, Zoe stuck her head out of the kitchen and glanced up the hall just as the pocket door slid open. Her younger sister, Lillian, slipped out and shut the door behind her. Despite the noise the arrival of the sheriff had made, Lillian tiptoed barefooted.

"Hi, Sis," Lillian whispered, throwing her arms around Zoe. "How's Ethan?"

"Holding his own. It's good to see you, Lil. Is Rory in there, too?"

"Yeah. We got in kind of late. You were already asleep."

"Well, come on into the kitchen. There's coffee on."

"I'm going to head upstairs for a shower first. I'll be down shortly." She turned for the stairs, took a look, and tiptoed back to Zoe.

"There's someone on the window seat," Lillian reported.

"Piper."

"When did she get here?"

"I have no idea."

39

By the time Zoe returned to the kitchen, Sheriff Tuttle was holding forth on the only time he had ever drawn his weapon.

"Yup," he said, in between two bites that made a doughnut disappear, "it was against my own deputy! Never meant to use it, but the man was just a bit drunk. It was the only way to get through to him."

He made a token gesture of standing as Zoe entered the room. Both Jennifer and Miriam exchanged a glance. Kip studied the countertop, her back to the room.

"Did Mr. Prescott here tell you we were working together?" Sheriff Tuttle asked as he shoved another doughnut into his mouth. "Had a big sting going, too. This guy here was doing all the dirty work. Hard to believe he's the same guy, if you want to know the truth. But I guess he's got to act the part. You tell them, Mr. Prescott."

Clearly uncomfortable, Andrew said, "Ah, I know we're in the most trustworthy of company here, Sheriff, and I know nothing we say will go beyond this room, but I am still hoping to resume the operation once the dust settles. If you don't mind, I'd rather not discuss it."

"You're right, absolutely right," Tuttle agreed. "I wouldn't mind seeing a big drug operation busted in an election year. For a while there, I worried that these kinds of things were happening in Feller County. And Bickle County, too. But remember, we've got a major north-south interstate running through our midsection, and plenty of outsiders come and go. Mr. Prescott can tell you, he's busted these types all over the state. It doesn't mean our own citizens are criminals, but it's sure easy for outsiders to get in and push all kinds of drugs, I'll tell you."

Another Kergulin, Zoe's sister Rory wandered into the kitchen in front of her brother Rob, just as Shep Tuttle was winding down.

"Hey, everybody," Rory yawned. "How's Ethan?"

While Miriam filled them in, Tuttle turned to Zoe. "Just how many siblings do you have, Miss Zoe?"

"There are ten of us," Zoe said, prepared for the usual reaction. "Not counting partners and kids."

"Nice Catholic family, huh?" Tuttle smiled as if the question had originated deep in his intellect.

"Nice Jewish family," Rob supplied, reaching around Zoe for a doughnut.

"McKenna's not a Jewish name."

"Our name's not McKenna," Rob pointed out.

"Ethan's from a mixed marriage," Miriam confided.

"Isn't that interesting?" Tuttle smiled tentatively, clearly perplexed. He picked up his hat. "Well, I must say, I don't meet too many Jews around here."

"Just hang around, Sheriff," Rob offered expansively.

"Well, I'll certainly remember that," Tuttle said as he stood and started for the hallway. "As I was saying, Miss Zoe, you just call me if there's anything my department or I can do. We'll be glad to help."

"Thanks, Sheriff," Zoe said, accepting the business card he handed her as he passed.

At the sound of the closing front door, Andrew lowered his head into the circle of his arms. Raising it again, he said, "I feel as if I should apologize for him. He pulls that dumb act all the time, but the more I witness it, the more convinced I am that it's not an act.

"I mean, look at his department and look at Ethan's. The people on your force don't make excuses, do they, Detective Randolph? From what I've seen, with the same kind of limited resources, Sheriff McKenna has managed to get special FBI training not only for himself but also for all of his top staff. There's no comparison between Bickle and Feller Counties. Bickle is the much more professional force."

41

Rob raised his chin in a movement Andrew already recognized from Zoe's behavior. "That's because Ethan is a professional," Rob said, "not a politician."

Jennifer Randolph nodded. "It's true. He was appointed to the position originally, you know. He didn't go looking for it. He just wanted to be a good cop." Under the guise of wiping her mouth with a napkin, she took a quick swipe at her eyes. "It's what he wants for all of us."

If she hadn't been caught shoplifting, Ren wasn't sure she would have told the police anything at all. Talking certainly hadn't been her plan. She had pictured herself braving tortures like the ones she'd seen on videos. The hero always took it. Fire, beating, even gunshots—the hero would do no more than wince or grunt and would never betray the information that was supposed to be protected.

Ren thought her secret would be like that. She thought she would be brave and steadfast and not tell, no matter what they did to her.

But as soon as she was arrested, she blurted out everything. She could have kicked herself. She was such a loser!

It started in the variety store, with the manager insisting on calling the police when he caught her shoplifting. All she'd taken was a greeting card. It was a stupid card, with a too-cute frog on the front, and inside was some stupid joke about kissing princes. She didn't even want the card. As soon as the manager caught her, she tried to pay for the thing. It wasn't that she didn't have the money.

She couldn't even say why she had stolen it. She didn't even have anyone to send it to.

Usually, whenever she was caught, the manager simply called her mother. Who would then show up, enraged, drive Ren home, and make her promise never to do it again. It was a shock to have this guy call the police.

As if that weren't bad enough, they arrested her. Even when she sniffled and began to cry, they handcuffed her and put her in the back of the patrol car.

She suspected that the man her mother had married had maybe talked to all the shopkeepers in Russell Creek and promised them some reward if only they would call the police the next time they caught Ren shoplifting. Not that there were many merchants who allowed her into their stores anymore.

The last time she'd been to the mall, one of the security guards had wagged his finger at her and told her the security service had her picture posted on the wall in the room where they had all of their monitors. That way, they could pick her out as soon as she walked into the mall, and then they could keep her in sight, no matter where she went.

Hot tears rolled down her cheeks and bounced onto the denim of her jeans. She was miserable, and she was cold. She should have zipped up her leather jacket before the police put the cuffs on her. They'd given her a chance to do it, but she had declined. In truth, the zipper was shot, and she didn't know how to get it fixed. The day was damp and cold, and Ren shivered in her misery.

She wondered if she should be calling a lawyer. The only lawyer she knew was the one her mother always used. His name was Albert Priory, which Ren suspected was a made-up name. She didn't like him—with his white shirt cuffs and his heavy-lidded eyes and the mustache that always seemed too short.

Even if she'd wanted to call him, she had no idea how to go

about asking for help from him or any lawyer. How would she pay for one? She had almost twenty-five dollars in her pocket, but she doubted that would go far with the services she needed.

In frustration, she kicked at the back of the driver's seat. The cop riding in the passenger seat turned around and stared at her through the grill that divided the front seat from the back. If Ren had thought she had the slightest chance of gathering enough spit in her dry mouth, she would have tried hawking a big one at the guy.

"Stop it, Ms. Bertram," he told her, stern-faced. "You don't want to make more trouble for yourself, believe me."

She didn't stop. She kicked again. She couldn't have stopped if she'd wanted to.

The driver said, "That's it," and pulled over.

They were just passing through the university area. Students were out on the sidewalks. Some of them glanced curiously toward the police car. At least the siren wasn't on. That would have drawn even more attention.

Billy Johns worked at a gas station not far from the university. What if he happened to be passing by, maybe test-driving someone's car, and he saw her sitting in the back of a police car? What would he think she might be saying?

Or, even worse, what if her mother's husband was around somewhere? If he saw her, he'd smile. He'd tell the officers he'd deal with her, not her mother. Then he would. He'd make the police send her to some juvenile facility, the way he was always threatening to. And much as she hated her home life, Ren knew that she would hate juvie even more.

"You can't stop here!" she told the officers. "You have to take me to jail!"

"You can go the rest of the way in the paddy wagon," the guy in the passenger seat said. "In there, you can kick as much as you like. Or, maybe we'll just restrain your legs, too. We can do that, you know. We'll just wait here until the paddy wagon comes."

"No," Ren said, feeling how quickly her heart was beating. "I have a statement to make." She hadn't watched all of those police shows for nothing.

"Yes, I have a statement to make," she repeated. "I saw the sheriff and that deputy get shot. I did! I'm a witness. You have to take me to the station so I can make a statement."

"You saw the shooting?" the deputy asked with an unbelieving half-smile. "Right. And I saw a pig fly, just this morning."

"I did!" Ren insisted. "I saw the two men who did it! I know about the blue cap, too!"

"What blue cap?"

"Call in," the driver told him. "Check out her story."

They placed Ren in a room with a table and a bunch of chairs. There were no windows, but she could hear the thunder, which had begun just after they'd started driving again.

The cops who'd picked her up disappeared. The one in the room with her was nicer. The tag on his shirt said his name was Kendall Ondean. It was a funny name, but Ren decided he looked kind of cute. His hair was on the long side, and he had a scar that divided his right eyebrow, making her want to look at him.

Ren tried to tell him her story, but he wouldn't allow it. He told her to hold onto it until the proper people had arrived.

The door opened, and another uniformed officer, this one a woman, said, "Kendall, the mother is on her way. So is Albert Priory, her attorney. They'll be here in about an hour. Agent Gordon will be available by then."

Kendall Ondean nodded and thanked the woman. Ren wondered whether he minded being stuck with her for another hour.

She certainly didn't like the idea of either her mother or her mother's lawyer coming to be with her. At least there was no word that her mother's husband was coming, too.

"How about I order us a pizza?" Kendall asked. "I didn't get to have lunch, and I'm kind of hungry. How about you?"

She smiled at him. She'd skipped school right before lunch period. She'd meant to get something to eat after she'd stopped in the variety store.

"Okay. Lots of cheese."

"Just what I was going to order!" he declared.

"Renata lies," her mother said. "It's what Renata does. She's lying to you now."

Ren didn't have to look up to know that her mother had every hair in place, every facial pore filled with just the right touch of makeup. Her mother was perfectly at ease in any social situation, even one set in a police station. Blinking furiously, Ren played with the broken zipper on her jacket.

Libby Gordon was with the FBI. She was dressed in a dark suit and a white shirt, which certainly made her look like the FBI in Ren's book. She had straight hair, not too long, turned under at the ends, brushing her jaw.

"Where did you see the cap, Renata?"

"I don't like the name Renata. I like to be called Ren. First, I saw it on the guy's head. The guy with the gun. He was wearing it when he ran down the lawn toward the car. But he ran so fast, it just fell off his head and landed on the lawn. He didn't even notice. Neither did the other guy."

"This is ridiculous!" Lila Mason declared. "Quizzing Renata about some cap is just fishing for stories! Those shootings happened Tuesday, right? Well, on Tuesday, Ren was at a school basketball game. She got home late. I had given her my permission to go. She could hardly have been watching the shooting and the basketball game at the same time, could she?"

The FBI agent calmly turned her gaze to Ren, who had suddenly spotted a big splatter of tomato sauce on her T-shirt. She couldn't seem to eat without getting food all over herself.

"Ren," the FBI agent said, "were you at the basketball game on Tuesday?"

"If my mother says I was, then I guess I was. We all know my mother doesn't lie." Ren was proud of the way she met Libby Gordon's eyes straight on. Lying took practice and a certain swagger. Ren knew she could look any adult in the eye and spout a load of bull. Those were just about the only times she had much confidence in herself.

"Where were you when you saw the blue cap fall on the lawn?"

There was no way Ren was going to tell the truth about her hiding place under the big tree. "I was at the edge of the woods, I guess. Not out in the meadow by the creek, yet."

"What were you doing there, Ren?"

"I was looking for this albino deer. Kids at school say they've seen her. She was born last year. So, I thought if I was really still, maybe I'd see her, too." There really was talk of an albino deer. Kids wanted to kill it. Ren didn't much care if she ever saw it, alive or dead.

"Did you see it?"

"No."

"Oh, please!" Ren's mother interjected. "Renata lies, I tell you! She wasn't sitting in the meadow, and she didn't see a deer or a cap. She must have read about the cap in the paper or heard it on TV."

"Now, Lila, let the officer ask her questions," Albert Priory said, placing his hand over her hand.

Lila Mason jerked away at his touch. "Stop it, Albert! I don't need coddling! Renata's lying. I know it, and so do you!"

"Ms. Mason," Agent Gordon said, "the information about that cap has been withheld from the media."

"Then Renata heard it from someone else! Besides, that cap could have been lying on the lawn all winter! You don't know!"

Ren leaned forward, wanting to be ready, not sure when the FBI agent would send a question back her way.

"We do know, Ms. Mason. It poured earlier in the day, soaking the ground. Then the rain stopped for a while. After the shooting, there was a slight drizzle. If the cap had been on the lawn all winter, or even all day, it would have been soaked from the rain. It was slightly damp. That's all."

The FBI agent blinked several times, as if to punctuate her statement. Then she turned away from Ren's mother.

"Ren," Agent Gordon asked, "how close is that spot where you were watching for the deer to the place where you saw the men running toward their car?"

"Just across the creek," Ren said with a shrug. "I don't know how far it is. Not too far."

"Did you get a good look at the two men who ran down the lawn?"

Ren shrugged again. "Good enough, I guess."

"Did you recognize either one of them?"

Calmly meeting the Agent Gordon's piercing gaze, Ren replied, "No." How could she possibly tell the roomful of people the truth about that?

"Would you recognize them if you saw them again?"

"I don't know. Maybe." Ren's eyes fell back to the broken zipper.

"Could you describe the men?"

Ren shrugged. "If you mean draw a picture of them, I don't think so."

"How tall were they? Was the man with the cap taller than the other one?"

Ren breathed hard, as if perplexed. "I don't know. Maybe."

"What race were they, Ren?"

Another shrug. "White, I guess."

"Build? Heavier or lighter than Mr. Priory here?"

"Well, they weren't wearing suits. It's hard to tell!"

"What were they wearing, then?"

"I don't know. Jeans, I guess. And parkas."

"Did you know Rosalyn Fitzgerald?"

"Not to talk to, but I'd seen her over there once or twice."

"Ms. Mason," the FBI agent said, turning back to Ren's mother, "is the Fitzgerald farmhouse visible from your house?"

Ren's mother's eyebrows drew together, and her lips pursed. "Certainly not! Our home is in the middle of twenty secluded acres. It's not even visible from the road. We can't see any neighbors, and they certainly cannot see us."

"How close is your land to the Fitzgerald home?"

Lila Mason's eyes widened, and she sighed. "Well, until this shooting, I certainly had no idea they were neighbors! The creek marks the boundary of our land on that side."

Like a tennis match in which you never knew when your opponent might spike the ball past you, Ren found herself on her toes. The questions were coming so quickly, she was afraid she would blurt out something she didn't want to say. She'd have to be very careful.

The short man who had come into the room with the FBI agent sat scribbling furiously and unobtrusively in a corner. Libby Gordon never had to ask him to clarify anything or repeat anything she had said. Ren was in a state very close to awe.

"Ren, do you know Rosalyn Fitzgerald's husband, Kirk?"

Shaking her head in reply, Ren looked at the tabletop, suddenly afraid to talk.

"For the record, Ren Bertram shook her head. Does that mean you don't know Kirk Fitzgerald, Ren?"

"I don't know him," Ren croaked.

"Would you know him to see him?"

"I guess."

"Was he one of the two men you saw running down the front lawn of Rosalyn Fitzgerald's house on Tuesday afternoon?"

"No." Pulled up from the depths of her, Ren was surprised to hear herself amend, "Ma'am."

"Did you know Rosalyn or Kirk Fitzgerald, Ms. Mason?"

"They're hardly of our social circle, Ms. Gordon!" Ren's mother said in a tone that made Ren want to cringe, crawl under the table, and stay there.

"It's Agent Gordon, if you please, Ms. Mason. Ren, do you know Sheriff McKenna?"

Ren snorted a laugh. "Duh. He's the sheriff, isn't he? Everyone in Bickle County knows him."

"Do you know him personally, Ren?"

"I've talked to him a few times, I guess," Ren answered, remembering the last time the sheriff had deliberately stopped his car, crossed the street to where she stood, and then just shot the breeze with her, acting as if he really was interested in what she had to say. She had proudly walked away from him, not willing to believe he was just being friendly with her—like she was someone worthy—but desperately wanting to.

"Did you see him drive down the road with Rosalyn?"

"Well, I saw the sheriff's car go by. He's the only one who has a white Blazer so I knew it had to be him. I didn't see her, but since the road goes right to her house, I figured she was in the car with him."

"Did you see either one of them again?"

"Uh-uh. I heard the gunshots, and then I saw the two guys running. That's when the hat fell on the lawn."

"What did the gunshots sound like?"

"Fireworks. A whole bunch in a row. At first, that's what I thought they were." A nervous smile flickered across Ren's lips. She had almost said, "we" instead of "I." Maybe her lips had even begun to form the word. "I didn't realize they were gunshots until I saw those two guys."

"Who was with you, Ren?" The FBI agent's voice suddenly became softer, more concerned. Ren knew better than to fall for that trick.

"No one." The girl's face had grown impassive as stone. She wasn't about to confess that she had long conversations with an imagined Billy Johns.

"There was someone else there with you."

Eyes falling to the stain on her shirt, Ren said, "TupTup."

"Oh, my God, Albert! We packed TupTup away with her blankie!" Ren's mother looked stricken.

Ren's face had gone beet red. She could feel the heat of it, but she had been boxed in. She had to give something away to satisfy all the questions. "TupTup is my imaginary friend," she explained haltingly. "I've known her since I can remember."

"Renata, you're fourteen! Don't you remember when we agreed to put TupTup away?"

Saying nothing, Ren played with the broken zipper on her jacket. Maybe TupTup hadn't been with her the day Rosalyn Fitzgerald died, but she still came around sometimes, especially at night, when Ren simply needed some company. TupTup hadn't liked being shut up in the attic, no matter how nice her mother said it was up there with the scrap of blanket Ren hadn't wanted to give up, either.

Maybe it was just the embarrassment of the confession, or maybe it was the absurdity of picturing the FBI agent trying to interview an invisible, imaginary friend, but Ren began to laugh. She laughed until she couldn't stop, until big, fat tears rolled down her face and landed on her worn leather jacket. She laughed until she could taste the pizza like a burp on her tongue, until she wanted to throw it all up right in the middle of the table. When she couldn't laugh anymore, she just kept crying.

"Wipe your nose, Ren," she heard after a while. Through bleary eyes, Ren looked up to see Libby Gordon at her shoulder, shoving some napkins toward her.

Obligingly, Ren took them. They were rough, and it chafed her nose to blow into them, but at least that waterfall of tears had stopped. Ren had no idea where that had come from. It had gushed from her with no warning, like a water pipe suddenly bursting.

She stifled a snort at the image of her nose exploding with steam that would spread so quickly, no one in the room would have a chance to escape.

Sitting back down, Libby Gordon gave Ren a minute more to compose herself. Then she asked, "Did you see the vehicle or vehicles the men were driving?"

As she nodded vigorously, forgetting to monitor every word that slipped out of her mouth, Ren said, "I sure did. A white Toyota pickup truck. I know the license number, too. Want to know what it is?"

She rattled off the number while her mother cried out, "Oh, please! Enough of this! Don't you know that she's doing what she always does?"

"What is it, Lila?" Albert Priory asked solicitously, leaning toward her.

Ren felt like clamping her hands over her mouth. She never should have said a word about the white Toyota pickup. She might as well just throw herself in jail. She didn't need any cops to lock her up. She could do a perfectly fine job of that on her own.

"When you check that license number," Ren's mother said, her lips a thin line breaking the set of her jaw, "you'll find it belongs to my nephew, Ellis Anton. And if you check further, you'll find that when Ren reports a crime, which she does often, she always manages to reveal that her cousin's truck was involved somehow. I can assure you, Agent Gordon, that my nephew is a law-abiding citizen. He works for his father's software company. My brother, who is Ellis's dad, is Joseph Anton, the founder of Antonetics, the biggest software firm in West Virginia. He's remaking the state in a technological image. That's his slogan. I'm sure you've heard of it?"

"Was your cousin, Ellis Anton, at Rosalyn Fitzgerald's house the afternoon of the shooting, Ren?" Agent Gordon asked her.

Miserably, Ren shook her head. "No."

"What do you have against your cousin, Ren?"

"Nothing," Ren mumbled.

"Why did you say that his pickup truck was parked by the creek?"

Ren shrugged. In a small voice, she heard herself say, "I guess I just thought it would be funny."

"Terrific sense of humor!" Lila Mason blurted angrily. "She tries to make trouble for the one person she should be emulating."

"You like getting your cousin into trouble?" Agent Gordon asked calmly.

Nodding, Ren shrugged again and sniffled. "He's so perfect. I just thought it would be funny. I did see the car that was parked at the creek, though. I didn't see the license number, but I did see the car!"

If her mother hadn't said, "Ren, you know you didn't! Stop lying!" Ren might have told the truth. Instead, she found herself saying, "It was a BMW! I didn't get the license number, but I'll bet there aren't many of those around."

"It's her cousin's car," Lila Mason wearily explained. "He owns it and the truck."

Libby Gordon looked at her watch. "Well, Ren, I would like to continue this, but I have a previous appointment that I'm already late for. Ms. Mason, would you object to Ren being interviewed again, not only with me, but also with a trained psychologist?"

"I certainly would object!" Lila Mason said. "You're trying to blame me because my daughter lies! She's lazy, and she wants constant attention. If those traits are my fault, then you might as well arrest me!"

"No one's trying to blame you for anything, Ms. Mason. We have established that Ren lies. A psychologist might be able to help us understand when Ren tells the truth. I'm trying to solve a shooting. I think Ren may be an important witness. It will be vital for us to know when she's lying and when she's not."

"Renata is lying about everything," Ren's mother said, biting off each word in very controlled anger. "She was at a basketball game on Tuesday afternoon. She was not at the creek, looking for deer. If my attorney and I have anything to do with it, you won't ever see my daughter again!"

The sun was nowhere near peeking out, but Zoe found herself blinking as soon as she stepped into the dismal grayness that was passing for daylight outside the hospital. Pulling her zipper higher, she tucked her chin into the gap between jacket and neck.

By her side, her niece Piper quickly wiped away tears. "Why is he frowning so much, Aunt Z? Do you think he's in terrible pain? And he keeps moving all the time. It's like he's trying to get out of bed, but he just can't get the leverage. It doesn't seem like it's Ethan there." A fresh cascade of tears leaked from her eyes.

"Miriam says it's all a good sign," Zoe said, not for the first time. They stepped off the curb and threaded their way around puddles and across the crowded parking lot to Zoe's car. "Yesterday, he wasn't moving at all. It was as if he had been thrown overboard. He sank like an anchor to the bottom of the ocean. Today though, he's started to swim toward the surface, far above him. It's going to take him a while, Piper, but he's on his way."

"Oh, that reminds me. Eric called just before we left. He's

rented one of those big vacation homes on wheels to drive Ethan's parents here. He said he didn't think his dad would be comfortable in a regular car because he'd recently had heart surgery. Did you know that? Anyway, they're on their way. I said I'd tell you. He thought they'd probably arrive tomorrow night sometime, barring any problems. Do you think he'll be able to get that boat of a vehicle down your driveway?"

"No, but he knows that. He'll probably tow a car. Or maybe he'll just go over to the McKenna farm. He'll decide when he gets here."

"Look! There's Kendall Ondean!" Piper waved to the man crossing the parking lot toward them.

Kendall and Piper had met at Ethan's winter picnic a couple of months earlier. They had spent quite a bit of time conferring, first over the punch, and then, as the evening wore on, in a quiet corner. Zoe had forgotten all about it and didn't even know if the two had kept in touch.

"Hi, Kendall!" Piper smiled.

The young deputy sheriff beamed engagingly in return, then dipped his head as he greeted Zoe. "How's Ethan doing? We've all been told not to even try to visit him, and the FBI sure isn't sharing anything they know."

"He's coming along, Kendall," Zoe said.

"He's in a coma," Piper added.

His expression almost fearful, Kendall confessed, "I found him, Zoe. It was like nothing I've ever seen before."

Tears pooled in his eyes, and he hastily swiped at them with his thumb. "My dad had been trying to reach Ethan and couldn't. That just doesn't happen. The sheriff is always in touch, either through the radio or his cell phone. Anyway, I was out that way, and I got the call to tell Ethan he'd broken his cell phone again. He's done that a couple of times, you know. No one thought it might have been what it was. We would have been out there a whole lot quicker if we'd suspected what had happened. I just think, if I'd only been faster then . . ."

"Rosalyn Fitzgerald would still be dead, Kendall," Zoe said. "And you saved Ethan's life. You were just as quick as you needed to be."

He nodded morosely, not quite believing her. Then his expression changed. "I almost forgot. I got sent out here to find you. I didn't expect to find you, too, Piper. I would've volunteered for the job if I'd known you were here. Oh, not that I wouldn't be pleased to talk to you alone, Zoe, but—"

"Who sent you to find me, Kendall?" Zoe interrupted, her intention only partly to save him from himself.

"Agent Gordon, from the FBI. She's taken over Ethan's office, turned it upside down. It's really strange to go in there now. She wants to see you at three. I tried you at home first, then the hospital. They wouldn't tell me whether or not you were here, so that's why I drove on over."

"Three? It's almost that now. Let's find a phone, Piper."

"Why don't you just go, Aunt Z? I can hang around and wait until Uncle David's ready to go back to your place. I'll hitch a ride with him."

"I'll be glad to take you," Kendall offered, on cue. "I'm off duty now. Maybe we could stop for a bite somewhere?"

Like a child hiding a piece of delicious candy in her mouth, Piper smiled at both of her companions. She'd gotten exactly what she'd wished for.

Even without the too-exuberant or too-subdued greetings Zoe heard from the deputy sheriffs as she entered the station, the place would have felt off-kilter. She saw the exchanged glances that she wasn't meant to notice, took note of the pursed lips that couldn't find the words to form, and peripherally caught the sympathetic eyes as she turned her back.

"Tell Ethan we miss him and hope he's back real soon," everyone seemed to say.

It was Chickie Ondean, Kendall's father, who took her to a small room by the front desk. Furnished with only a desk and a chair, the bare walls made even whispered conversation sound harsh. Words delivered in a regular tone of voice echoed like an out-of-sync carillon.

Zoe had never been in the room before, wasn't even aware of its existence.

Reading her thoughts, Chickie explained, "It's our getaway room. Really, it's for visiting parole officers or police from other localities or whoever needs a quiet place to do some paperwork. Sometimes, we all take a turn in here just to get the reports finished. No distractions, you know.

"What I wanted to tell you is that the FBI agent who's conducting this investigation has taken over Ethan's office. Nobody offered it to her. She just took it."

Zoe nodded. "It is the logical place for her to be, Chickie."

"I feel like we're violating his trust, letting her put her things all over the place. It's not right. She's making it seem like he's not coming back."

"It's okay, Chickie. I know it's Ethan's office."

"Well, I just wanted to warn you. No one is happy about it, but we have no say with Ethan not here. And she's a fed." He looked Zoe square in the eye and shrugged. "What can you do?"

Zoe was quick to discover she had spoken too quickly. It turned out it was not okay. For one thing, Ethan's door was locked. Never before had she found his door locked. It might be closed now and then, but never, during the day, was it locked.

Knocking produced no results, so Zoe slid down the wall and sat on the carpet. Ethan's office was in the middle of the back wall of the building. A corner office would have given him more windows and a more commanding status position, but what he had wanted was a better view of his organization.

Zoe checked the clock jutting out from the corridor wall, greeted passing deputies, and rested her eyes. In her mind, she pictured Rosalyn Fitzgerald's house, going over the grounds again, seeing where the shooter had stood, considering what the shooter had done once it was assumed both Ethan McKenna and Rosalyn Fitzgerald were dead.

"Hey, you," whispered a familiar voice, close by her ear. "There's no loitering in the halls. Want to get yourself arrested?"

The merest touch of a smile brushed Zoe's lips, and she yawned, stretching broadly. If anyone had asked, she would have denied being able to nap during the day, but she had, indeed, nodded off for several seconds, if not several minutes.

"Hey, yourself," she greeted Willa, yawning again. "Why are you hanging out here?"

The reporter knelt beside her, purse and briefcase blocking the hall. "I had to attend a briefing."

Her glance taking in her friend's usually impeccable grooming, Zoe asked, "Are you dirtying your suit just for me?"

Willa brushed at imaginary specks on her skirt, and she and Zoe hauled themselves to their feet. "This is linen, too. You know what it'll look like even if I don't spend all day deliberately trying to wrinkle it. But I had to buy it. Don't you think the color of my skin just warms the ecru?"

"Ecru," Zoe repeated, as if learning a foreign word. "It's not the color of your skin, Willa. It's you. Anything you wear suddenly gets transformed to greatness."

"Only next to your oh-so-casual look. What are you doing here?"

"I've been summoned by the great and powerful Oz." She nodded toward the door. "Libby Gordon, the FBI agent, has taken over Ethan's office." She squinted at the clock. It was after three-thirty. "What kind of a briefing were you at?"

"Ed West, state police. Have you ever seen this guy? Picture Joe Friday, the cop from 'Dragnet.' Without the charm."

A flicker of a smile preceded Zoe's question. "What did you learn?"

"Nothing. Worthless rehash. One reporter from one of the tabloids wanted to know if Ethan and Rosalyn were fully clothed."

Raising her hands as if to ward off a blow, Zoe quickly said, "Don't tell me. I shouldn't have asked. I don't want to know."

For a moment, Willa silently studied her friend. Then she said, "You should have a press conference, babe. Or at least release a statement. The family should have something to say."

"We do. 'No comment.'"

"But why? If someone accused my cousin of having an affair with a subordinate, I'd sure want to have my say. Especially if it was an especially close cousin."

Zoe shook her head. "People will think whatever they want to, no matter what I say."

"People will think whatever they want to after they've heard all sides," Willa insisted.

"There are no sides in this case, Willa. There are only the facts, which no one officially investigating the thing seems too eager to uncover."

"Can I quote you on that?"

"No."

"You didn't say it was off the record."

"Then print it. I can't stop you."

"But you'll never talk to me again, hmm? Tell me what you know, at least. You're always so closed-mouthed. How can we be better friends unless we share?"

Zoe smiled tiredly at Willa's persistence. "Know a better way to bust up a friendship than to blab someone else's secrets or suspicions to the world?"

"Come on, Zoe. My editor knows we're friends. Just give me one thing you're thinking. Even off the record. Who do you think did the shooting?"

"Off the record, huh? Okay. I don't know."

"You have your suspicions, right? You have to know that the police under Ethan's management are suspects, right? They're all feeling scrutinized right now. What do you think about that?"

"I think Agent Gordon is walking down the hall at this very moment. I've got to go, Willa. You take care."

More than invaded and occupied, Ethan's office had been effectively leveled, and another one built over the top of the debris.

Zoe sat, not in the old wooden chair she had always occupied across from Ethan, but in an overstuffed monstrosity that smelled as if it had been pulled from under a stack of dusty books. Her usual chair was barely visible under cardboard boxes stuffed with the things that made Ethan's job important to him.

All of the certificates and awards Ethan had received from various community groups had been removed from the walls and packed away. The knickknacks that usually littered his desk—from the little rubber Yoda figurine to the group photo of the basketball team he coached, from the much-doodled-upon blotter to the mousepad that sported a photo of the dog he'd loved as a kid—had all disappeared.

Except for the desk chair, which still seemed to be indented where Ethan's head rested when he leaned back to make phone calls or to think, all traces of the sheriff had been deliberately removed.

Despite herself, as she sat in the chair, rank with its mildewy smell, Zoe found herself taking in the immense changes in the office and saying, "Ethan *is* coming back to this office."

Libby Gordon quickly sat down and interlocked her hands on top of the new, unmarked blotter, ruefully saying, "I should have instructed the front desk to have you meet me elsewhere. It's bound to be a shock, seeing what looks like Ethan McKenna being physically removed from this office. I assure you, however, that I only needed the room. I took Polaroids of everything so I'll be able to put things back exactly as they were when the case is wrapped up. In the meantime, though, I needed a well-equipped office, and this one was available.

"I do apologize, however, for my tardiness. I was interviewing a possible witness, and the time got away from me. I certainly had no intention of keeping you waiting, Ms. Kergulin."

Zoe nodded, not having registered much of Agent Gordon's apology except the part about the witness. "Did you learn anything about who might have done the shooting?"

"No." Libby Gordon opened the top drawer of Ethan's desk and pulled out a pad of paper and a pen. From the glimpse Zoe got, she knew that the desk, too, had been cleared out. Ethan always rummaged through that top drawer; everything seemed to get shoved in there.

"Now, Ms. Kergulin," Agent Gordon continued, "we're hoping for some clarification and assistance from you. I'm sure I can count on your help."

"If there are any questions I didn't answer at the hospital, ask away. I'll do the best I can."

"Several of the files on Sheriff McKenna's computer are locked with a password. Would you happen to know how to get into any of them?"

"No."

"Don't you want to hear which files they are?"

"It wouldn't matter. I assume they're personnel records or case files. Ethan and I may be close, but he'd never tell me how to get into files that are none of my business."

"You know we have people with the expertise to get past the passwords. It would save us time and money if you'd provide them, however."

If Libby Gordon saw the answering lift of Zoe's chin, she did not acknowledge it. "As I've stated, Agent Gordon, I am not privy to any passwords on Ethan's computer."

"Tell me this, then. Have any of the people who work in this building ever confided in you or complained to you about Sheriff McKenna?"

Zoe's jaws clamped together so strongly she could have cracked walnuts with her teeth. Consciously slowing her breathing, she gave herself several more seconds before she said, "As a matter of fact, at Ethan's winter picnic last year, there were several deputies who confided in me. One—I think it was Kendall Ondean—told me he thought he was so lucky to be a Bickle County cop and to have Ethan McKenna as a mentor. Jennifer Randolph confided that she was nominating Ethan as Sheriff of the Year for some law enforcement organization's award. And I believe one of the veteran officers once whispered that he knew of no other law enforcement organization that was better run."

There was a long slow intake of breath on the other side of the desk. "There's no reason for us to be antagonists, Ms. Kergulin. I want to find out who shot your cousin as much as you do. Are you aware of anyone in this building who ever made a threat toward Ethan McKenna? Did he ever tell you about any threats he might have received?"

"I know of no one who might have made a threat against Ethan."

"Did he ever complain to you about any of his subordinates?"

"No. If Ethan had a problem with anyone, he took care of it."

"Can you give me an example?"

"Not really. It was none of my business, so if there were problems, I never would have been told. The only thing I do remember him saying once was that he thought one of the deputies, and he didn't name any names, would really benefit from FBI training, but he didn't have the money in that year's budget. He was thinking about what he could do to find the money or raise it to send that officer to the National Academy."

Libby Gordon tilted her head. "You expect me to believe that Ethan McKenna is some kind of a saint?"

"He's not a saint. There's nothing miraculous in what he does. He's a mensh, that's all. A good person. You may not believe me because you don't meet a lot of people like him in your line of work, Agent Gordon. But he's genuine. Ask anyone who knows him. I'm not attempting to be obtuse. I'm simply describing the person I know."

"Then let me ask you this. Are there any people employed by the Bickle County Sheriff's Department that you would suspect of having it in for Ethan McKenna? For whatever reason, real or imagined?"

Obligingly, Zoe gave it some thought. At last, she shook her head. "There's no one I can think of."

"You know, Chickie Ondean is poised to step into the sheriff's job. He's older than the sheriff by more than a few years. Hasn't he ever mentioned how hard it is to be under the thumb of a younger man?"

"Chickie Ondean?" Zoe barked with a semblance of a laugh. "Chickie would do anything for Ethan. He doesn't want to be sheriff! He knows the paperwork and the prodding it takes. Chickie's waiting for June second, seven years from now, when he can retire streamside and fish all day long."

The pen Libby Gordon had been doodling with was carefully placed on the paper. Again, she folded her hands together. "Do you know Kirk Fitzgerald?"

"Rosalyn's husband? No."

"Did Sheriff McKenna ever mention his name?"

"Not that I can recall."

"Did Ethan McKenna tell you he was having an affair with Rosalyn Fitzgerald?"

Zoe sighed as she looked at Agent Gordon's short, but sculpted, fingernails. A layer of clear glaze had been applied to each one.

"I told you 'no' at the hospital, and my answer hasn't changed. Ethan would never get involved with a subordinate. Besides, as Ethan will be happy to tell you once he can, he's gay."

"Perhaps bisexual would be a better description. He was married once, wasn't he?"

"When I was in junior high, the baseball team my brother coached needed a right fielder. I had grown up hearing stories about Roberto Clemente, the best baseball player ever to take up bat or glove. I'd read every book I could find on him. I wished so desperately I could have seen him play. In my mind, I wanted to be just like him. So I told my brother I'd gladly play right field. Know what? I didn't fit in the position. Simply holding the title didn't make me an athlete."

Zoe watched as Libby Gordon blinked rapidly several times. Her jaw moved back and forth before she spoke. "Thank you for coming in, Ms. Kergulin. I know you won't mind if we find we have to call on you for further questions."

Zoe stood, glad to be free of the enveloping odor of the chair. "Look, Agent Gordon, I know you're only trying to do your job.

Truthfully, though, there's no way I can imagine that anyone who knows Ethan would ever want to shoot him. Logically, however, I do know it's possible, and that whoever left him for dead might come back to try to finish the job. That's why Ethan's brother has hired round-the-clock private security at the hospital. Only family is getting in to see him."

"I'm sure one of the other sheriff's departments nearby or even the state police would gladly help you out."

"We don't know about them, either, do we?"

"It's probably a wise move," Libby Gordon said, tearing off the top sheet of paper and neatly placing the clean pad back in the top drawer of the desk.

Ethan had given up his rental house in Russell Creek and moved back to the family farm. The main house was occupied by Zoe's brother and family, and Ethan had chosen the isolated old house where the McKennas' cook and her family had lived.

Almost a mile past the main entrance to the farm, a narrow asphalt road forked off to the right. Twenty yards down the road was an open gate. The short drive beyond that curved around a ridge and dropped down to the cozy house squatting beside a large pond. In summer, ducks and geese set up a racket when any visitors arrived, but the solitude Zoe found as she parked the car seemed entirely appropriate to Ethan's absence.

Skeletons of trees stood bleakly against the fading sky, a slight wind tugging at their exposed branches. Rocks huddled in the bare front yard, and two picnic tables and benches looked as if they'd burrowed into the sand for warmth. Even the big, windowless garage, Ethan's addition to the landscape, hunched stark and cold.

Zoe knew she shouldn't be there. Libby Gordon had neglected to ask if she had a key for Ethan's house, but Zoe knew enough about murder investigations to have turned the key over without question, even though the place was not, as far as anyone knew, a crime scene.

But it wasn't that easy for her to relinquish anything that was Ethan's, let alone a stake in finding who had shot him and killed his deputy.

She had spent the day with Ethan, watching him ever so slowly plod his way toward consciousness. By evening, he opened his eyes on request, although there was absolutely no expression on his face, no spark in his eyes. Occasionally, but perhaps randomly, he would squeeze a hand when asked. Zoe preferred to liken the response to that of her cats—if they felt like doing something, they did it when she asked. Other times, they had better things to think about and simply ignored her.

Brothers and sisters had come and gone, the security detail had changed, but Zoe had not been able to tear herself away from Ethan's bedside. It seemed to her that if she waited just another minute, he would emerge from the coma like a swimmer breaking the surface of a pool, gasping for air and invigorated with the accomplishment.

It was the nagging thought that there might be blatant clues at her cousin's house that finally pulled Zoe away from the hospital. Once she put the car in park and turned off the engine, the idea of violating Ethan's domain suddenly weighed heavily on her. With ten children in her own family, Zoe knew very well the value of privacy. She leaned against the car door and studied the two big picture windows, one on either side of the front door. The venetian blinds were shut against prying eyes, even in this rural setting.

She sighed, considering.

After several ponderous minutes, she strode to the door. Ethan had given her a key for a reason. She figured this was it.

When Zoe unlocked the door and stepped inside, she stood still, letting her eyes wander around the living room and, like a person meeting a dog for the first time, letting the house check her out, adjust to her presence.

The place looked very much as it always looked, with newspapers scattered across the couch and coffee table, an empty glass on the arm of a chair, and the handset to the cordless phone adrift on the cushions, next to the TV remote.

In the quickening dusk, Zoe went from room to room. Upstairs, she opened the closet in Ethan's bedroom and simply stood there for a moment, catching a whiff of him. Then she began her search in earnest, parting the hangers, examining the floor, the paneling in the back, and the top shelf of the closet—seeking some clue he might have hidden, something that would tell her why he had been a target.

Turning to the rest of the room, she tried looking under the unmade bed, under the pillows, and in and behind the dresser drawers. She found nothing.

The smaller bedroom, where Ethan kept his computer, was tidier than the rest of the house, but not by much. Ethan could access files at work from his home, but Zoe truly had no idea what his password might be. Idly, she booted up the computer, hoping—foolishly, she knew, but hoping nevertheless—that she would miraculously come upon a file labeled, "For Zoe, in the event I am shot."

The small closet in that bedroom concealed not only the attic steps but also a bathrobe on the back of the door. Terry cloth and blue, it smelled of a not unpleasant blend of pipe tobacco. Zoe smiled quizzically. Apparently, there was something Ethan had chosen not to tell her. Holding a fold of the robe in one hand, she tried to picture its owner. No face materialized.

It had to be a relatively new relationship, Zoe figured, or she would have heard about him by now. Not long enough, by everything she had learned, for a new romance to turn sour, for a suspicious lover to become a jealous murderer.

In the middle of wrestling with herself over whether or not she had the right to go through a stranger's pockets, she heard tires on the gravel parking area. Shoulders tensed, she hit the light switch and tiptoed to the window. Lifting the blind enough to peek outside, she strafed the ground with her gaze.

There was another car out there, parked beside her own. Zoe held her breath until she recognized Jennifer Randolph, the plainclothes detective, unfolding herself from the driver's seat.

Clattering downstairs, Zoe pulled open the front door just as Jennifer knocked.

"I thought that was your car," Jennifer said. "I've been doing a drive-by almost every night on my way home, just to make sure the place is secure. Is everything okay?"

"Fine," Zoe nodded. "I thought I might pick up a few things for Ethan, some touches of home."

"How's he doing?"

"He's coming along."

"We sure miss him. Tell him that." Jennifer scuffed the toe of her shoe against the doorjamb. "Things really aren't going well without him. You'd think we'd just keep functioning the way we always have, but nothing's the same."

The thought of discussing Ethan in his empty house was too close to the image of talking about him over his unconscious body. Zoe could not do it.

"How about I buy you a beer?" Zoe suggested, nodding back toward the refrigerator. "We could sit outside. If you don't mind."

Despite the evening chill, they settled side by side on a bench at one of the picnic tables, the wood of the table poking the women in the back as they watched the breeze play on the steel-gray pond.

Jennifer said, "The real trouble with having the FBI around all the time is that you're constantly reminded that the people you work with, who only last week were colleagues, are now suspects. I don't know who I can trust anymore. You know, Ethan has worked long and hard to get us to function as a team, but since the shooting, I'm lost. We all are. It's such a strange sensation, not knowing who the enemy might be."

"Jennifer, everyone in the department knows where Ethan lives, don't they?"

With a shrug, Jennifer replied, "I guess so. He invited us all here for the winter picnic. How many people do you know who plan cookouts for December? No ants, Ethan said. No flies. Everyone was cold, but we had fun, too . . ." Her voice trailed off and took her wistful smile with it. She shrugged. "Ethan's always been very generous with all of us."

Zoe rested her elbows on the table behind her. "You know what doesn't make sense?"

"The whole thing."

"Besides that. You just said everyone in the sheriff's department was here in December, right?"

"Sure. Well, everyone not on duty was here."

Zoe continued, "So everyone knows where he lives. If the intent was to get Ethan, then why not do it here?"

"Unless the intent was to get Rosalyn," Jennifer pointed out. "Or both of them. You know, even if they weren't having a thing together, some people might have construed it that way. I mean, he did spend a lot of time with her."

Zoe breathed deeply, feeling the damp cold. "Do you think

there's anyone on the force who hates the two of them that much?"

Jennifer shook her head. "That's where I hit a snag. The truth is, it's got to be someone, doesn't it? Someone who knows where Rosalyn lived, someone who knew Ethan was going to be driving her home that day."

She took a long swig from the beer bottle and shivered with a sudden chill. The look she cast on Zoe was pale and bleak. "That pretty much boils down to someone I work with, don't you think?"

Zoe's frustration was only increased by her lack of access to Rosalyn Fitzgerald's family. Her husband, Kirk, was still being held in protective custody. At least that was what the FBI called it. What had appeared to be a potential alibi on Tuesday had deteriorated into a misshapen sieve by Friday morning.

With some degree of excitement, Willa had called her the previous night, soon after Zoe's return from Ethan's house.

"Get this, babe," Willa had said, triumph clear in her tone as if she had uncovered the story herself instead of merely passed it along. "Rosalyn's husband was supposed to be conducting a seminar all day Tuesday in Wheeling. He was there Tuesday morning, but Tuesday afternoon, he had a subordinate lead the session. There's no one from that afternoon session who remembers seeing him after lunch. He insists he watched from the back of the room."

"Willa, is there any evidence that he drove or flew back to Russell Creek that afternoon? It would be cutting things very close, if he left around noon. Could he fly here in that amount of time? Assuming a plane was ready to go, and he could pick up a car, drive out to his home, shoot his wife and Ethan, then repeat the steps in reverse?"

"The police are checking things out is all I know. I did look at available flights. I don't think he could logistically do it. However, he could have driven all the way. You know people do ninety on the highways."

"What time does his alibi pick up again? Was he back in Wheeling Tuesday evening?"

"Yeah. That's where the local police found him to notify him of his wife's death."

Zoe had grown silent, turning over possibilities. "Is there any evidence he was ever unfaithful to his wife, Willa?"

"Funny you should bring that up, Zoe." Her tone added, *especially when you can't believe it of Ethan*, but she did not give the thought voice. "It turns out he had an affair with his secretary last year. It lasted about two months, she says. She was the one who stepped forward and told the police. She insists, though, that he never, ever talked about hating his wife or wanting to see her dead. What makes you ask?"

"Because I'm wondering if anyone else might have been missing from that seminar for the afternoon session."

"Ooh, some female-someone, you mean! I like it. I mean, even if you could prove you were at the Hot Sheets Motel the afternoon your wife died, is it something you'd want to confess to the police? I have a friend on TV news in Wheeling. I'm going to call her right now. I'll let you know as soon as I hear anything."

Zoe had checked Rosalyn Fitzgerald's obituary in the paper. Her mother's name was Sharon Williams, and the sister was Carla

Williams. Both of them lived in Elkins. Friends would be received on Monday at the funeral home. Burial would be Tuesday. The wait was so long because the body had not yet been released by the medical examiner's office.

All week, Zoe had dialed the number listed for Sharon Williams in the phone book. There had been no machine and no pickup until first thing Saturday morning. Although Sharon Williams had refused to speak to any reporters, she did agree to see the cousin of the Bickle County sheriff on Sunday morning at eleven.

It was not Zoe's first circuit of the property belonging to Rosalyn and Kirk Fitzgerald. Nor was it the first time the rain pounded down so heavily that it felt to Zoe as if she tramped around under a waterfall. The likelihood was that any evidence the official investigators might have missed would surely have washed away by now. Nonetheless, Zoe could not stop her search. Surely, somewhere on the property, there must be something that pointed to the identity of the shooter.

As the rain continued to beat out a staccato rhythm on the hood and back of her jacket, Zoe once again felt as if someone were watching her. Jerking up her head, her eyes swept the nearby outbuildings, skimmed over her car, parked in the public parking area, and flew across the creek.

There was no sign of anyone, but she was absolutely certain someone was nearby. Zoe suddenly realized what a target she was. Not only was she alone, with no one knowing where she was, but she was standing in the middle of the grassy expanse of the front yard, her rain jacket a bull's-eye for any shooter who might be hidden nearby. Had the killer returned? Or, Zoe thought as she headed for the shelter of one of the outbuildings, deliberately slowing her pace to a saunter despite the frantic warnings from the panicked adrenaline coursing through her, had the possible witness that Agent Libby Gordon alluded to come back?

Zoe discerned movement under the blue spruce across the stream. Someone crawled out from beneath its branches, a heavy-set young woman who froze when she realized Zoe had spotted her. The young woman stared at her the way her cat, Chocolate Pudding, used to do when she'd first come to live in Zoe's big Queen Anne. The cat had been abused by someone, and in the beginning, when Zoe had accidentally gotten too close or had happened to raise her voice when talking to Ethan in another room, the cat would take several quick steps away, then stop and cringe, knowing escape was futile, awaiting the blows certain to fall.

Zoe took a step away from the shelter she had almost reached. "Hello!" she called out. "I'd like to speak to you!"

At Zoe's first movement toward the stream, the young woman found her feet. She took off in the opposite direction, her unzipped leather jacket and long hair swaying behind her.

By the time the young woman reached the shelter of the trees at the edge of the clearing, Zoe was already splashing across the creek. She ignored the water that immediately hit her at knee level, but was unable to dismiss the frigid temperature of the stuff that seemed to send an icy siphon into her and suck her breath away.

She fought the deceptive current, thrashing through the water, and grabbed a handful of grasses on the far bank to help pull herself out. As she passed the spruce, the unmistakable odor of marijuana hit her nostrils.

Her quarry had already disappeared into the woods, but perhaps someone else lingered under the branches of the tree. Zoe pulled aside the heavy lower limbs and discovered a neat hideaway, nearly dry in the downpour. The lowest limbs had been trimmed, and the drape of higher branches created a tentlike space. A blanket was wadded up and stuffed into a plastic grocery sack by the tree's base. Although Zoe's eye detected no visible evidence of marijuana, the area under the tree reeked with the scent of it.

As the storm let up a little, Zoe was suddenly aware of how icy her legs felt, how numb her feet.

"Get away from there right now!" someone screamed close by.

Startled, Zoe turned to face the young woman, who had returned, perhaps drawn by the lack of continued pursuit or by Zoe's curiosity about her hideout. She was younger than Zoe had first thought, maybe thirteen or fourteen. She had a rock in her fist, although she had not cocked her arm. Her long, brown hair hung lank and wet, a streak of stark red standing out like blood beside her pale face.

"That's my tree! It's on my property! You're trespassing!"

"I wanted to talk to you," Zoe said, taking a step forward on legs that suddenly felt wooden. "Why are you spying on Rosalyn Fitzgerald's house?"

"Are you a cop?" The young woman's face turned suspicious and surly.

"No."

"Then who are you?"

"An interested party. Why is the deputy's house so riveting?"

The young woman shrugged. "It was like watching TV. Only I couldn't change the channel." She laughed with a sound that trailed off into a snicker.

"What have you seen over there?"

Languidly, the young woman blinked. "The police already asked me if I saw the shooting. I said yeah, but my mother told them I lie."

"Do you lie?"

"Every chance I get." It was a proud boast.

"My name's Zoe." She stuck out a cold hand. "Zoe Kergulin."

A grip that challenged met hers. "Mine's Ren Bertram. Don't say, 'Why, you don't look like a little bird.'"

"That's a beautiful name. Why would I make fun of your name?"

"Everyone does. It wouldn't be the first time."

Zoe buried her hands in her jacket pockets. Her legs were so frigid they were leaching warmth from the rest of her. "Why did you tell the police you'd seen the shooting, Ren?"

"Are you a reporter? Will I be on TV?"

"I'm not a reporter. I'm an investigator. Mostly I'm here because my cousin was shot over there. He's the sheriff. Ethan McKenna."

"Your cousin? Too bad for you."

"What do you mean by that?"

The young woman rubbed at a stain on her sweatshirt. "Nothing."

"Did you see the shooting, Ren?"

The young woman solemnly nodded. "I saw everything. First, Rosalyn and the other guy, your cousin, were doing it in the backseat. Then, this guy wearing a mask walked up to the car and pointed his gun inside. Blam!"

She made a pistol out of forefinger and thumb, recoiled with the imaginary shot, and then blew on the tip of her finger. She smiled benignly at Zoe.

"Where were you when you saw all this?"

"Where I was today! Where do you think? Under the tree. I can see all kinds of things there, and people usually don't see me. It's a big tree."

Zoe flexed her knees and wiggled her toes, trying to retain at least a hint of feeling. Her legs quivered like aspen leaves in a breeze. "Look over there now, Ren. The drive curves after it passes by your spruce. Then the lawn rises, and that line of hemlocks blocks your view. Even a taller car like the sheriff's Blazer would be hidden. I don't think you could have seen anything that happened at the car from your vantage point under the spruce."

"Maybe I moved. Maybe I went over here, to this rock!" Ren stomped across the wet grass, suddenly pitched forward, and went down.

Before Zoe could stumble to her side, Ren was up again, one hand to her right knee. "I tore my damn jeans! See what you made me do?"

"Even from that rock, you wouldn't have been able to see the car or the shooting," Zoe pointed out.

"Well, I didn't want to get too close or I'd get shot, too! I'm not a fool!"

"How about the other times you watched Rosalyn Fitzgerald's house?" Zoe's teeth chattered, despite her best efforts. "What did you see then?"

"Lots of stuff," Ren answered airily. "I knew her whole life, practically."

"What did the gunman look like?"

"Didn't I tell you he was wearing a mask? How would I know what he looked like?"

"What did the mask look like?"

Ren shrugged disgruntledly. "Like a mask."

"What color was his hair?"

"I don't know. He had on a knitted cap. It was one of those dark blue ones. Ooh, then it fell off! Let me think. What color was his hair?"

"Renata?" came a faint call through the trees. "Renata!"

"Oh, no!" Ren grimaced. "That's my mother. I've got to go. Ow!"

She had taken one step and doubled over, clutching for her bloodied knee. "Could you help me? I need to get home. Ow!"

It seemed obvious to Zoe that Ren was not in terrible pain. If it gave her more opportunity to question Ren, however, Zoe was more than willing to play along. Already, there was new information that could be verified or discounted among the tales Ren had conveyed.

She offered her arm to Ren, who grabbed it and leaned heavily on Zoe's shoulder.

They hobbled together into the woods, warmth returning to Zoe's limbs as she forced herself forward. The sound of dead, tenacious leaves rattling on otherwise bare trees caused Zoe to look up. Sleet was falling, with tiny, icy pellets bouncing on the ground around them.

Although Ren relaxed her death grip on Zoe's shoulder as they made their way through the trees, as soon as a clearing appeared before them, the younger woman once again threw herself onto the support of the older woman.

Stomping into view was a short, slight woman wearing a tightly cinched trench coat and carrying an umbrella. The spokes of the umbrella snagged the tree limbs as she entered the woods and came toward Zoe and Ren.

"I fell, Mother," Ren said, making an exaggerated yowl as she grabbed her knee. "Maybe I need some painkillers or something."

The woman ignored her daughter and studied Zoe intently. "I don't believe I know you. Do you have business here?"

"I'm Zoe Kergulin, Ms. Bertram. I—"

"It's Mason," Ren's mother interrupted. "Lila Mason. Renata's father and I are divorced. I've remarried."

"Ms. Mason, Sheriff McKenna is my cousin. I'm trying to find out who shot him. I was hoping your daughter might be able to help me."

"What in the world makes you think Renata would know anything about that?" The woman's free hand fluttered near her throat.

"I saw her just now as I was at Rosalyn Fitzgerald's house. Maybe she saw something the afternoon of the shooting."

"I was looking for that albino deer again, Mother. You don't think someone's shot it, do you?" Ren asked, standing upright as she forgot about her wound.

"Nonsense!" Lila Mason spat out. "Ren was at the school basketball game. The police have already checked it out."

Her mouth pursed, belying her distaste at what she found herself proposing. "You're both going to catch your deaths out here. You'd better come inside and warm up. My house is just there."

The woman stepped aside at the clearing, moving her umbrella and revealing a three-story Queen Anne replica with turrets, towers, and custom-made windows. An enclosed deck with a gazebo on the end stood closest to the women. Zoe counted no fewer than five chimneys poking toward the gray sky.

They trudged toward the front of the house, where a double door opened to a hall medieval in size, with a cathedral ceiling that disappeared into skylights three stories above. Despite the draperies and area rugs, couches and upholstered chairs, the tile floor echoed footsteps to the surrounding windows, bouncing all sounds back down again.

Zoe could not stop her head from swiveling. Opulence shouted from the fixtures and furnishings. With the amount of mahogany, oak, and gold trim all around, the effect was overwhelming rather than stunning. And the absence of books made the room seem stark, despite the overstuffed plushiness of the decorating.

Observing Zoe's amazement, Ren smiled falsely. "This is just a little something we threw together. What do you think?"

"Oh, Renata!" Her mother shook her head. "It's this way to the kitchen and the laundry room, Ms. uh—"

"Kergulin. Zoe will do fine."

The kitchen in Ren's house was unlike anything Zoe had seen

before, except in restaurants. There were two stoves, one a professional six-burner, the other an Aga, the British stove popular with Americans of a certain income. Two refrigerators sat side by side. An island in the middle of the floor was shaped in an ell, with a small refrigerator under one side. The countertops were all a polished, dark granite. Three sinks were scattered around the room.

Custom-made tiles marched across the floor and up the walls, framing windows and doors. A computer sat on a desk in an alcove in one corner, abutted by a TV and VCR.

"Do you think blood will permanently stain this floor?" Ren asked as she squeezed her injured knee.

"Stop it, Renata!" Lila scolded. "You go upstairs and get out of those wet clothes. Right now!"

"She only yells because she loves me." Ren's smile was as sweet as it was false.

When Ren had flounced upstairs, via a back stairway from the kitchen, Lila shook her head. "Let me throw your things in the dryer, Zoe. There's a shower in the laundry, if you'd like. You do look as if you've caught a chill. Meantime, while your clothes dry, I could get you a blanket to wrap up in and a cup of tea."

The water was hot, and Zoe let the steam rise around her in humid clouds, steeping her like a tea bag, until the shivering stopped, and she was warmed through. A shower had never been so delightful.

Afterward, she wrapped herself in the quilt that had been left for her on top of the washing machine, and she stepped back into the kitchen.

As she bustled about the huge kitchen, her heels clacking against the tile floor, Lila Mason acknowledged Zoe's return with a nod and said, "Renata does lie, you know. She probably told you so herself. She's quite proud of it."

Pulling out a high stool at the island, Zoe situated herself behind a placemat Ren's mother had put there. "Why does she lie, Ms. Mason?"

Without stopping her fluttering movements as she set water on to boil, rinsed a teapot, and sorted through at least a cupboardful of various boxes of teas, Lila Mason answered without turning around. "She's always been that way. From the time she was just a little girl."

"Did something happen then?"

Her hand clenching a box of Darjeeling, Lila Mason slowly turned to Zoe. "Do you have children?"

"No."

"Then how would you know what children do or don't do? I told you Renata has always been this way. Are you suggesting there's some deficiency in me as a mother?"

Zoe's eyes narrowed, and she fought a sudden urge to lift her hands in surrender. "Ms. Mason, I implied no such thing. I'm simply stymied to come up with a reason why Ren would say she saw the shooting when she didn't."

"For attention, of course. Why else does a child do anything? My daughter thinks she has never had enough attention. Even when raising her was all I did, it was never enough. She always wanted more. So she's constantly coming up with schemes to try to get everyone to notice her. I am sorry about what's happened to your cousin, Zoe, but I assure you, if you think Renata has any answers for you, you've come to the wrong well for water."

Zoe let her eyes wander around the huge kitchen. "This is some house," she observed, not exactly intending a compliment.

"We call it The Cottage, the same way the British underplay their own mansions," Lila Mason declared proudly. "It's the most expensive house in the development, you know. Almost a million dollars! My brother, Joseph Anton, made it all possible. Maybe you've heard of him?" In response to a slight raising of Zoe's shoulders, Lila Mason continued, "Well, he's a whiz, simply a whiz with computers. He started his own company years ago, and my husband and I got in on the ground floor. Three years ago, one of the big software companies bought Joe out, and we all got rich. Joe stayed on as a consultant. We all still have a hand in the business."

For a brief moment, Lila Mason lost herself contemplating a huge stone in a ring on her right hand. Her smile disappeared as she again made eye contact with Zoe. "You know, I have tried to get Renata some help. All the psychologists and psychiatrists in a three-county area tell me they can't do a thing without her cooperation. When she's in their offices, all she wants to do is make up stories. Until she decides to let us, no one can do a thing to help her."

Zoe sipped her tea, using a hand barely released from the warm folds of the quilt. The airs and histrionics of her host had reminded her of a saying her mother had been fond of quoting: God doesn't think too much of money. Just look at the people she gives it to.

"You don't have children," Lila was saying, "so you wouldn't know the heartache a mother goes through, worrying about her child."

"I'm driving my mother into an early grave!" Ren declared, dramatically smacking the back of her hand to her forehead as she burst into the kitchen wearing bright purple sweats. "Luckily," she stage-whispered to Zoe in a voice quite loud enough for her mother to hear, "she'll get to go in a luxury car!"

Zoe took another sip of the flowery tea. Her middle was chilled again, but it was not from the cold.

Ren searched cupboards until she found a bag of pretzels.

Opening it, she sat beside Zoe at the island countertop. "There were two guys, you know," she confided, offering the bag to Zoe. "Only one was shooting, but there were two guys. Did I forget to tell you that?"

"Oh, Renata!" her mother exclaimed, rolling her eyes. "I think we've heard quite enough of that story. Zoe won't know you're only kidding."

"I'm perfectly serious, Mother."

After swallowing a very small sip of the scalding tea, Lila placed her cup on the counter and said, "My daughter was in school on Tuesday afternoon, Zoe. Wasn't that the day the sheriff and the deputy were shot? The police have already talked to Renata, you know. Just this morning, I got a call from my lawyer, who had been in touch with the FBI. It seems that Billy Johns, no less, has corroborated the fact that Renata was at the basketball game, where she was supposed to be. He's the captain of the football team, you know. If he says Renata was sitting in front of him for the entire basketball game, then you can be certain that's where she was. His friends all say the same. So, you see, my daughter is lying again. You simply cannot believe her, Zoe."

"What's your last name again, Zoe?" Ren asked her.

"Kergulin."

"What kind of name is Kergulin, anyway?"

"The same kind as Bertram," Zoe smiled, refusing to be needled, which was what she thought Ren was trying to do. "A family name. What was the second man doing, Ren?"

"He was arguing with the first guy. After the shooting, that's when I saw them. I didn't see him before that. After they finished arguing, they got in the truck that was parked right where your car is today, and they turned around and drove away." Ren nodded, as if verifying her story, and chomped loudly on a pretzel.

"Did you recognize either of the men?"

87

As if taken aback, Ren blinked eyes that had suddenly grown huge. "How would I know two murderers?"

"Renata!" Her mother chided. "Zoe, I must ask you to stop. Egging her on only makes her exaggerations worse."

"Don't you want to know if I got the license number of the truck? I did! And it was a white Toyota pickup." Ren settled her shoulders and smiled without showing her teeth. "I already told the police. A kind of rusty white Toyota pickup. Maybe five or six years old. The license number is—"

"Enough!" Lila Mason cried, slamming her open palm down on the countertop. She brushed the side of her cup on the down-swing, and tea sloshed over the lip, puddling on the polished granite surface. "Go to your room this minute, Renata!"

Flouncing to her feet, Ren sneered. "Good! Music videos are on, and I planned to watch anyway."

Using the awkward situation as an opportunity to rescue her clothes from the dryer, Zoe quickly slipped out of the room and into the warm garments.

Ren and Lila had both disappeared by the time Zoe returned. If there was a back door out of the house from the kitchen, she could not find it. Zoe made her way back through the long hall to the great room, where she pulled open the huge front door and stepped outside.

The world had turned white while she'd been otherwise occupied. Snowflakes the size of moths sprouted from the indistinct gray sky and fell around Zoe with an almost audible thud. Already, more than an inch of snow camouflaged the ground.

Behind Zoe, the front door opened again. Lila hugged her arms, shivering. "Do you need a ride back to your car, Zoe? I could have one of the servants drive you."

"No, thanks." Zoe wouldn't have turned down a ride from Lila Mason but was uncomfortable having the woman volunteer someone else for the job, even someone in her employ.

Zoe turned up the collar of her jacket, tightened the hood, and walked away briskly. From the edge of the woods, she turned back and looked at the place again. The house had windows radiant with fanlights, and even stained glass. It was certainly a thorough copy of a Queen Anne, the style of house Zoe proudly owned and admired herself, but try as she might, Zoe could find none of the charm of her home reflected in the image that sat on the perfectly landscaped lawn. And she couldn't even put a finger on what it was that was missing from the exterior of Ren's house that made it look so cold and clinical. Even three years empty, her house had beckoned. Lila Mason's did not.

Taking a last glance at the magazine-spread house, Zoe stuck her chin back into the collar of her jacket and pushed her way into the wet, snow-cloaked woods.

At the blue spruce, Zoe stopped and surveyed the view again. The top of the porch roof was visible, as was the lower end of the line of hemlocks where the shooter had stood.

Not relishing the deed, Zoe nonetheless dropped to her knees and crawled under the canopied lower branches of the tree. Inside the shelter of the boughs, the earth was not only free of snow but dry, too. The trimmed branches made it possible to sit comfortably or to lie flat. Through the branches, Zoe could still see the front lawn of Rosalyn Fitzgerald's house, along with part of the house.

The heavy odor of marijuana lingered among the spruce needles, disguising the smell of the tree itself.

Zoe took the blanket from the grocery sack and shook it out. It, too, smelled of marijuana, but there was nothing else hidden in the bag. She refolded the blanket and slipped it back into the plastic, replacing it against the trunk, as it had been.

As she sat quietly beneath the tree, she could feel the weight of the snow hanging on the branches above her. The sound of water rustling over rocks in the stream was a constant presence, but Zoe thought it was not loud enough to drown out the sound of a heated argument even some distance away.

With the cold beginning to seep through her jeans, Zoe imagined two men coming down Rosalyn Fitzgerald's lawn, one of them holding a smoking gun, both of them angry. Why?

She shook her head. It could all be a story Ren had concocted. Even though it was all she had, Zoe knew she had to question the veracity of the account Ren had recited.

Taking a last look at the upper windows of the house across the creek, Zoe crawled out from under the tree with renewed determination. She forded the stream again, gasping despite herself as the icy water rose above her knees. As long as she could keep her feet beneath her, she knew she'd be fine.

Quaking more than shivering by the time she reached the bank where her car was parked, she slipped and slid, making progress up to the parking area by slow degrees, scrabbling on all fours most of the time.

On level ground again, she stumbled to her car. Her hands were icy, and she needed both of them to turn the key in the lock. She fumbled with the ignition but managed to get the car started. Then she slammed the door behind her and locked it, even though—as far as she could tell—she was alone.

She turned the heat up all the way, flexing her toes and her fingers. It took several long minutes before she felt up to the task of cleaning off the windows. Back in the car, she carefully turned around and headed toward Russell Creek.

In the case of the back roads of West Virginia, flat stretches are the exception rather than the rule, but the snow was falling so quickly and so heavily that rises and dips leveled out. There were times when Zoe could not find the road at all.

Tension urged her to hunch over the wheel, but common sense kept forcing her to ease her back against her seat so her eyes could take in all the clues to where the pavement might be. Signs and fences helped, although when the old Chevy fishtailed and scraped barbed wire, it was the wavy line of her own tire tracks that allowed Zoe to point her way back toward the road.

Trees bent under the burden of their sudden load, and branches bowed before Zoe like unctuous and obsequious waiters showing her the way to a not particularly good table.

In most places, the tracks behind her were the only ones that broke the monotony of white. Once she reached the ramp to the interstate, however, tire-flattened snow delineated at least the right lane of the highway. Despite the absence of snowplows, Zoe was able to pick up speed and cruise into Russell Creek at an average of twenty-five miles per hour.

Main streets in Russell Creek were relatively clear, and most had been cindered, although the snow was still falling so thickly that bare pavement was a rare sight, even right behind a plow.

Zoe skidded into the parking lot at the sheriff's office, narrowly missing the dumpster. She took a deep breath, the first one she'd had since she'd left Ren Bertram and her mother. It felt so good, she took another.

Inside, Kendall Ondean was at the front desk with the phone to one ear and five lights flashing under his poised fingertips. He waved at Zoe in the comfortable, offhanded way he always did when she stopped by to see Ethan.

She acknowledged his greeting and strolled down the hall in her usual manner, but she was not heading for Ethan's office. It was Jennifer Randolph's cubicle she was looking for.

In the hallway, however, she met Andrew Prescott, the state narcotics agent.

"Zoe!" he greeted her. "How's Ethan? How are you?"

"He's coming along," she said. "How are things going here?"

He took a pull from the can of cola in his hand and looked down the empty corridor behind him as he said, "The snow's got everyone out on the streets. Fender benders all over the place. Power outages. Was it bad out there?"

She nodded. "Early spring snowstorms. Tomorrow it'll probably hit sixty degrees, and the snow will be gone without a trace."

"Zoe," Andrew said, glancing down the corridor again as he lowered his voice, "have you noticed a car following you? Have you seen any sign of someone watching your movements?"

"What do you mean?"

He exhaled audibly and frowned, as if considering. Then he said, "There are rumors flying all over the place about a stranger in the county who's showing up where he shouldn't be. Like at Rosalyn Fitzgerald's house."

"I was just out there. I didn't see anyone."

"Oh Zoe, you shouldn't be out there, period, but if you go, you should have some backup. Please, promise you'll ask me or someone else to go with you if the need arises to return to that house."

"What's this stranger doing?"

"No one knows. He's an African-American, about six feet tall, and he drives a silver Jaguar."

"A Jaguar shouldn't be hard to spot in this county. It's probably the only one around. Why is he a suspect? Is it his skin color?"

Andrew's eyes widened. "Certainly not! Look, Zoe, I didn't want to tell you this, but the guy was also spotted nosing around Beverage. That's where your house is, isn't it? Chickie Ondean told me. Having been there, I can assure you that no one would be likely to stumble on the place. Why would a guy be sneaking around Rosalyn Fitzgerald's house and possibly looking for yours? Maybe he's trying to threaten you, Zoe."

She forced a laugh, although her stomach had acquired a lead weight. "Well, he's not going to do very well on Bickle County roads driving a Jaguar in this storm. And he's going to do even worse on my driveway. It's ungraded and full of potholes."

"Just be careful, please. Are you armed?"

"I can take care of myself, Andrew." Her mind was whirring, though, ticking off possible matches with former antagonists. Although Willa had assured her that every one of the people she might have suspected from her past was busy elsewhere, Zoe wondered if there was someone her friend had missed, someone she was overlooking, too.

"How about a bulletproof vest? You really should be wearing one. I could make sure you get one."

"Thanks, Andrew," Zoe said dismissively, "but I'm okay."

"I could be your unofficial bodyguard, at least for a few days. Look at it this way—it would give me something worthwhile to do. At least until I can go back to our sting. I hope we'll be able to tell Ethan real soon that it's all over. Reassembling the sting won't happen for a few days at best, so I'd be more than happy if you'd let me just hang around, unofficially. Who knows? Maybe we'll solve the case together."

"I'll let you know, Andrew. And thanks for the offer," Zoe said, finding that she had lowered her own voice in response to Andrew Prescott's volume. "Why are we whispering?"

Andrew took another look over his shoulder. "Sheriff Tuttle is here somewhere, and I just know he's looking for me to—"

"Well, there you are, Mr. Prescott! And Miss Zoe, too! What luck!" Shep Tuttle's voice boomed down the corridor. He smacked his hands together in anticipation as he hurried down the hallway toward his quarry.

"Miss Zoe," he continued, grinning avuncularly at Andrew's proximity to her, "I'm glad to see you and Mr. Prescott together. You make a fine-looking couple."

With a sudden lowering of his own voice, he continued, "Say, did you hear about that Rosalyn Fitzgerald's husband? It turns out he once threatened another police officer, back where he used to live in Virginia. How about that?

"And that's not all. There's another suspect in the shooting. Besides the husband, I mean. The FBI is keeping pretty tight-lipped about it, but there's a big black guy in a sports car who's been seen nosing around Bickle County. You keep your eyes open, Miss Zoe. I know I'm going to alert all of the Feller County deputies." He shook his head. "I'll tell you, this snow is doing us no favors. This guy could escape before we even have a chance to question him."

Zoe found Jennifer Randolph sitting in her cubicle, her ear to the phone. She motioned for Zoe to come in, hooking the visitor's chair with her foot and pointing with her forehead. Obligingly, Zoe slid into the seat.

Jennifer had tacked up magazine photographs of mountains on one wall of her cube. Formidable escarpments and jagged rocks were the dominant features on display. Zoe studied the pictures even as her ear tuned in to Jennifer's share of the conversation, which consisted of no more than acknowledgements that she heard or understood whatever the other person was saying.

At last, with a shake of her head, Jennifer hung up. She made a quick note and tucked the paper into an already crowded corner of her blotter before greeting Zoe. "How's Ethan?"

"He's coming along."

Jennifer stretched, and a smile took possession of her mouth as she studied Zoe's damp jeans, the dirt on her knees and hands, and the smudge across her cheek. "I have to say, Zoe, I like the look."

Realizing the state of her appearance for the first time, Zoe grinned. "It grows on you."

"Especially if you water it regularly. What can I do for you?"

"First, is it true that Kirk Fitzgerald threatened a police officer in Virginia?"

"Who told you that? Wait, I bet I know." Jennifer lowered her own voice. "Here's the rumor: Kirk Fitzgerald was involved with harassing a cop in Virginia. At the time, both the cop and Kirk were wooing a certain soon-to-be cop Kirk later married. It could have been a simple spat or the beginning of a pattern. Zoe, leave it up to the FBI to sort out."

"Okay. Is there any evidence that Kirk Fitzgerald made the trip across the state on Tuesday afternoon?"

Jennifer rolled her eyes and whispered fiercely, "Didn't I just tell you to let the FBI handle it?"

"The FBI can handle it. I just want to know if anything new has been uncovered about Kirk Fitzgerald."

With an audible exhale, Jennifer whispered, "Not as far as I've been able to learn. Now, is that it?"

"Jennifer, what can you tell me about Ren Bertram?"

Although she threw up her hands as if she'd never heard a more outrageous question, Jennifer sat forward to say, "She couldn't have seen anything, Zoe. She was at a school basketball game. I helped verify it."

"No, tell me about her before the shooting. Has she ever been in trouble?"

"Hoo," Jennifer said, waving her arms, leaning back in her chair, and crossing her long legs. "You don't know the half of it. That girl's been in trouble since the day she first breathed air. I don't even know where to begin. Her parents divorced when she was two or three, and then her dad split to parts unknown. Shortly after that, we got a call from Ren. What could she have been, four at the most? She said her mother wasn't there, and she was all alone. She said a bad man kept watching her, and she needed help. A deputy was dispatched, and the mother answered the door. It turns out the girl had been sent to her room for one reason or another, and she got lonely and decided to dial 911.

"Since then, we've all come to know her. She gets picked up at all hours. She always has a far-fetched story to tell about why she's out. We take her home. Her mom grounds her, and the next day Ren's back out hanging around the Dairy Delite at midnight.

"She's been picked up for shoplifting, for truancy, and for stealing her stepfather's car. There have never been any serious consequences, legal or otherwise. The family's one of the richest in Bickle County."

"How about involvement with drugs?"

Jennifer shrugged as she reached for a pencil. "She smokes marijuana. You can smell it on her usually, especially late at night, but she's never been busted for it, never been caught while she's in possession. As far as I know, that's it for drugs."

"Do you know how she does in school?"

The desk chair shifted as Jennifer sat forward and threw the pencil back onto some papers. "Hah! When she attends, you mean. Even when she's there, I don't think anything's getting in anymore. Her teachers don't have nice things to say about her."

"Friends?"

Sadly, Jennifer shook her head. "There's no one, at least as far as I know. You know how Ethan has been organizing evening activities for the kids with nowhere else to go? Well, she's never shown up, even though I know Ethan invited her. I think we'd all just fall over if she did come. Although, I should add, she has told her mother all about what she's done during those evening activities. She's a world-class liar, Zoe."

"Did she lie about there being a blue knitted cap found on Rosalyn Fitzgerald's front lawn?"

Jennifer's eyes widened. She glanced around the cubicle as if she could see through its walls. With a frown, she silently considered options. At last, while writing on a piece of scrap paper, she carefully said, "Oh, Zoe, you know I can't discuss specifics of any case with you. Don't ask me to cross that line."

Written on the paper she slid to the edge of the desk were the words, "Meet me at Richardson's Cafe in fifteen minutes."

"I debated about bringing along someone to take your statement," Jennifer said, swiping at snow on the shoulders of her jacket. She'd slid into the booth opposite Zoe and huddled over the table, leaning close, although there was no one else around them. "But geez, the consequences."

Richardson's Cafe was not a popular police hangout, which Zoe figured was why Jennifer had chosen it. It was conveniently located, just a block down the street from the county police station, but the windows were perpetually rain-stained, and the light from outside barely penetrated. The food was, at best, mediocre and tended to arrive tinged with gray, perhaps owing to poor light. Even the brightness of the snow outside did nothing to enliven the sickly contents of the ketchup bottle or make the napkin dispenser look anything but dirty.

Jennifer's eyes swept around the place again. "The FBI is letting us take little pieces of the investigation, but we're not privy to what the big picture looks like. I guess that's normal when you don't know if someone close by might be involved in the shooting. Still, it rankles.

"You know what's missing? Ethan. We never have to worry about the politics of any investigation. He handles all that stuff. But now, it's filtering down to everyone. And I don't know how to play the game, Zoe. Nor do I want to. I think most of us feel that way. So, we're lost. With the way the FBI and the state police are treating us, they don't trust us. So I'm wary of trusting them in return.

"Then you come with this story about the cap. And from Ren Bertram, of all people. I don't know who I could tell it to."

To overcome baring her confusion, Jennifer ducked her head and took a sip from one of the cups of coffee Zoe had ordered. Making a face, she reached for the sugar and generously poured in a few tablespoons.

"You didn't know that Ren knew about the cap?" Zoe asked in low tones. Jennifer's extreme and uncharacteristic nervous caution had leaked across the table. "Is it true, then?"

"Maybe she made a lucky guess."

The way she bit the words told Zoe that Jennifer didn't believe that any more than she did.

"Did you see the cap on the lawn when Ethan was shot?"

A reluctant nod was the answer. Staccato breaths filled the space between the two women until, her mind made up, Jennifer said, "I think someone told her. And I think that someone is Shep Tuttle."

"Shep Tuttle, the Feller County sheriff?"

Jennifer sighed. "Zoe, I don't know how much you know about him. Ethan's the one who always had to interact with him, but I'd heard rumors about how incompetent he is. At first, I didn't put much credence in them. I wish I had, though. The man is unbelievable.

"When I was thinking about going into law enforcement, I always heard there were two true things: one, Feller County's sheriff was a fool and a politician and nothing else; two, Bickle County's sheriff was corrupt. Take your pick.

"I considered just staying in the military. Then Ethan took over in Bickle County. Things turned around. Apparently though, nothing's changed in Feller County."

Zoe shook her head and found her own eyes quickly scanning the empty restaurant as she said, "But I don't see the connection between Ren Bertram, the cap, and Shep Tuttle."

Wearily, Jennifer nodded. "It's not far-fetched at all. He's been out there at Rosalyn's place giving interviews, explaining what happened. As if he has a clue! It would have been so easy for Ren, who, I'm told, spied on Rosalyn anyway, to overhear something that Sheriff Tuttle said."

"Why is Shep Tuttle involved at all? What's Feller County got to do with this shooting?"

Half of Jennifer's mouth frowned. "Because Rosalyn's house is practically right on the Feller County line. She lives—lived—in Bickle County, but when you're on the road leading to her house, you're in Feller County. So the FBI, in their infinite wisdom, involved the Feller County police."

"But, Jennifer, suppose Ren really did see what happened? Suppose she's not lying?"

The deputy snorted through a sip of her coffee. "That would be a first!"

Jennifer replaced her cup on the table, although her fingers lingered around the rim. "Look, Zoe, Kendall Ondean and I talked to Billy Johns. Ren had his name written in a notebook in her purse. It was on a page of doodles with hearts and things. It was found when she was picked up for something unrelated. You know who he is?"

Zoe shook her head as her eyebrows slid toward each other. Hadn't Lila Mason, Ren's mother, mentioned his name?

"He's the captain of the football team and the class president. And he's smart and handsome to boot. He's the kid every parent wishes they had. Billy confirmed that Ren was at the basketball game on Tuesday afternoon, just where her mom said she was. If Billy says he saw Ren, then he saw Ren. She's got to be lying about seeing that cap. She wasn't anywhere near Rosalyn's place on Tuesday afternoon, no matter what she says."

Zoe sipped her coffee, surprised to find it cool. "Jennifer, today I found Ren under that big blue spruce that's right across the stream from Rosalyn Fitzgerald's house. I think she must crawl under there regularly. The lower branches have been trimmed, and there's a blanket. Ren would have a great view of the front yard from under there. She could easily have seen someone lose a cap. But with the stream there, I'm not certain how much she'd be able to hear. The water isn't frozen, and it's pretty lively."

"Zoe, her story's already been checked. It's a lie. She was at the basketball game."

"She says she got the license plate number of the shooters. There were two men, not one. Did she tell you?"

A tired smile crept across Jennifer's face. She shook her head sadly as she extracted a notebook from her jacket pocket.

"Don't tell me," she instructed, flipping through pages. When she found what she'd been looking for, she read off a number.

Puzzlement in her expression, Zoe studied Jennifer's face.

Putting her hand to her head as if divining the information, the deputy sheriff added, "And it's a white Toyota pickup truck, isn't it? Kind of rusty?"

"Whose is it?" Zoe asked in disappointment, certain now that here was at least one of Ren's lies she hadn't been sharp enough to discern. "Shep Tuttle's?"

"No, try Ellis Anton."

"Ellis Anton? I heard that name today." Zoe turned pages in her own notebook.

"He's Lila Mason's nephew. Ren's cousin. Ren gives us his vehicle on a regular basis. If there's a hit and run anywhere in the county, if someone speeds past a school bus, if a bank is robbed, we get an anonymous phone call from Ren Bertram. Each time, she gives us that pickup truck and license plate number."

"So, she fooled me about the pickup. But the knitted cap, Jennifer. That can't be a lie."

"Forget it, Zoe. Someone let something slip. Ren's not stupid. She picked it up and ran with it. I'm warning you, the more you believe her, the bigger the story she'll tell."

"Why does she keep turning in her cousin?"

Jennifer shook her head. "I don't know. He's the heir apparent to the family money. They have big, big bucks. His parents are the reason Ren's family is so rich. Maybe he's the apple of his family's eye."

"Lila Mason did manage to point that out."

Laughing, Jennifer said, "Probably twenty or thirty times. My guess is that cousin Ellis is always being praised, and Ren just doesn't stack up very well next to him. I'm not sure there is any one reason why she makes so much trouble for him." She shrugged. "Because he's there."

"I'm grounded again, Billy," Ren told the snow. Her tears ran in icicles down her cheeks. She sniffled, shivering. It wasn't true that snow fell silently. She could hear each fat flake hit the various piles already covering the blue spruce. Gentle plops, like rose petals falling on a calm lake, sounded all around her.

The air was alive with the iridescence of snow landing. Ren knew how the flakes sparkled in the lights from her house, but under the spruce, all visible light came from the snow itself. Magical droplets she could catch on her tongue. If she swallowed enough of it, would she glow, too?

She laughed halfheartedly and continued to cry. Her cache of marijuana was safely hidden under the little snow that had managed to burrow between the tree's branches, but Ren was really too cold to retrieve it. If she stayed out much longer, there was a good chance she'd freeze to death. The thought was both frightening and welcoming. If she killed herself, even accidentally, she wouldn't be able to hurt anymore.

In spite of the damp chill, the air was getting warmer, and the snow was getting heavier. Soon, it would change back to rain—even the weather contributed to the sense of irony about her life. Just when she decided to freeze to death, the temperature rose.

All the forces of the universe lined up opposed to her. That woman named Zoe who'd said she was a cousin to the sheriff, she seemed interested enough in what Ren had to say, but Ren knew how easily professionals could fake that. There wasn't a single psychiatrist she'd been to who cared about her at all, but each one pretended to, just so her mother would pay them their big fees. Ren had no use for them, for any of them.

They all thought there was something wrong with her because she tried to tell the truth. At least in the beginning she had, but none of them wanted to hear it.

Ren sighed, but the sound was lost in the sighing of countless snowflakes settling aimlessly around her.

She felt a drop of water hit the top of her head. Looking up into the darkness intensified by layers and layers of white on the branches above her, Ren knew the rain and melting snow would soon dampen her shelter. Higher temperatures combined with a heavy snowfall were just about the only things that could make the blue spruce uninhabitable.

As she crawled out, the weighted branches touched her bare back where pants and sweatshirt parted. Ren shivered. She was tired of pretending she was so much bolder than she was. In truth, the world scared her silly. The marijuana didn't even help her stand it much anymore. If she simply fell down and stayed there, a frozen snow angel, maybe she still had time to die. With her luck, though, the changing precipitation would drown her. She'd be a laughingstock in death, as she feared to be in life.

Suddenly, Ren turned and looked back across the stream. Her eyes traveled longingly toward the dark yard. Maybe what she needed was more protection than fantasies offered. Maybe what she needed was a gun. Her mother didn't have a gun. Neither did that man she'd married, at least as far as Ren knew.

But there was a gun across the creek, a gun that had already killed Rosalyn Fitzgerald, and maybe the sheriff, too. Ren had seen exactly where the guy who'd lost the cap had thrown it. If only she could get her hands on it. If she had that gun, no one would dare not believe her, no matter what she said. And if she did decide to kill herself, maybe she could shoot someone else first. Having a gun would make that possible. For the first time all day, Ren smiled.

"I hear you're the star of the Falcons," Zoe said to the young man who filled her gas tank. She had deliberately chosen the full-service pump, planning to ask whoever came to point out Billy Johns to her. It was a lucky break that the attendant who strolled out was wearing a shirt with the gas station logo and the name "Billy" inscribed atop the pocket.

"I'm the quarterback, ma'am," he said deferentially. His blond hair glittered with red highlights, even on the overcast morning. Blue eyes beamed from a square, handsome face. "I don't think that makes me the star."

"That's not what I hear," Zoe said. She'd asked Jennifer Randolph for the scoop on Billy Johns. That was how she'd known where to find him on this drizzly Sunday. Snow had changed to rain overnight, and rain had tapered to drizzle. Temperatures hovered around forty, so although the heavy snowfall was undeniably melting, it wasn't shrinking quickly. Huge plowed drifts of blackened slush were piled unappetizingly at the far end of the station lot.

Zoe smiled at Billy Johns. "I've heard there are several colleges interested in you. It's pretty impressive for a junior to be as skilled an athlete as you are."

Besides talking to Jennifer, Zoe had visited the library and reviewed a few old copies of the *Russell Creek Bulletin*. It hadn't required much research. Just about every football game had been written up with a feature story on the high school's golden quarterback.

"I've been really lucky, ma'am. My team makes me look pretty good."

"Maybe you make them look good, too."

He blushed. "Can I check your oil, ma'am?"

"Yes, thanks." Zoe reached in the open door and pulled the hood release. "Do you play any other sports?"

After struggling to find the safety catch under the hood, Billy shook his head. "Not really, ma'am. The coach, he wanted me to concentrate on football. That's what I did. And sure enough, it looks like I just might get a scholarship out of the sport, especially if the team does as well next year. I've been real lucky." After a couple of minutes, he informed her, "Your oil's fine, ma'am. Nice and clean, too."

"Have you worked here long, Billy?"

"Oh, yeah. Ever since I turned sixteen. I've got to pay for gas and insurance for my own car. That was the deal my parents made with me."

A red Mustang drove into the station, looking freshly waxed and gleaming, despite the slushy condition of the roads. Billy grinned as he watched the car stop at the pump, and the pretty young woman behind the wheel smiled invitingly and waved.

"My girlfriend, Holly," Billy said with an aw-shucks dip of the head. He slammed shut the hood of Zoe's car and loped off toward the Mustang, shoving the bills Zoe had given him in his pocket without even looking at them. His broad shoulders belied his youth, but the hurried gait gave him away.

The young woman in the red car ran a hand over her hair and smiled even wider at Billy's approach.

Zoe drove away with a full tank of gas and a picture of Billy Johns that fit exactly with the description of the football star she'd read about in the paper. What reason could he possibly have had for lying about seeing Ren Bertram at a basketball game? He wouldn't have known her from school. He was a junior, she a lowly freshman. The surprising thing was that he had noticed Ren at all.

Of course, with that streak of brilliant red in her hair, Ren might very well be one who would stand out in a crowd.

Although she found no reason to doubt Billy Johns' story, experience had taught Zoe to check what could be checked and to double-check what couldn't.

It was Sunday, near noon, but she cruised over to the high school anyway. The place was deserted. The asphalt of the wide parking lot was unmarred by a single car or truck.

For a moment, Zoe let the car idle, stymied.

It had been a frustrating morning. She had driven to Elkins to see Sharon and Carla Williams, Rosalyn Fitzgerald's mother and sister. They told her Rosalyn had been a loving daughter and sibling, a good wife as far as they knew, and a darn good cop. It was still inconceivable that anyone could have killed her.

"She went to church regularly," Sharon Williams had confided proudly, as if that should tell Zoe everything she needed to know.

As for Kirk Fitzgerald? He'd been a model husband, they both agreed. Back when he was courting her, he'd been a little jealous of rival boyfriends, but since he'd won Rosalyn's affections, he'd settled down to be a wonderful guy. It was inconceivable to either of them that he'd had anything to do with the shootings.

After that, Zoe had stopped at the hospital to see Ethan. His blank eyes stared at her without expression or recognition, like a mannequin standing nude and unaffected in the biggest display window of a department store.

Several of the monitors had been disconnected, but they had not yet been removed, as if standing by, waiting to jump into the fray once again, if required.

Relieving her sister Rory, while her younger sibling went to grab a bite, Zoe sat quietly with Ethan, talking in low tones, sharing what she knew as she always did, her ear anticipating his reply.

Another operation on his shoulder was scheduled for early the next morning. That thought prompted her to call Ethan's brother to ask whether the security firm he had hired to stand guard at the hospital had encountered anyone besides reporters trying to sneak past them.

Eric checked while Zoe was still on the phone.

"One guy," Eric reported. "Tall, African-American. Well-dressed. When confronted, he refused to say anything. He simply turned and walked away."

"Did anyone get a name from him?" Zoe asked then, wondering if she had too easily dismissed the rumors ricocheting around the sheriff's office.

"No. The guy left, and there's no further report of him. I'll see if I can get something in more detail, and I'll let you know."

The parking lot was still empty as Zoe emerged from her reverie. She made a note to follow up with Eric sometime later and let her notebook droop dispiritedly to the empty seat beside her.

With a sudden inspiration, Zoe drove out of the school's parking lot and back onto the street, heading once more for the library.

Although the small county library closed early on Sundays, the university library Zoe frequented stayed open most days until after dark. Without worrying that she'd have to race against a clock, Zoe tucked up a chair at a computer and surfed for information. The Bickle County High School did have a web site of its own and, beneath an icon of a basketball net, Zoe found the school's schedule for that sport.

Tuesday's game had been against arch-rival Feller County. Following the highlighted clues, Zoe finally clicked on the page that showed the schedule for school activities on the local cable TV access channel. At seven that night, a rerun of Tuesday's basketball game against Feller County was scheduled.

Zoe checked the current time. It was ten to five. Swiveling slowly back and forth, Zoe chewed at the side of her thumb. She didn't have cable at her house. Hooking up an isolated house that sat a mile or more away from its nearest neighbors was prohibitively costly. But Ethan had different priorities. He had cable. Zoe quickly found herself driving out to his house again.

Uneasiness hit the moment she pulled up in front of Ethan's house. The trash cans beside the porch were both stuffed full, parts of plastic bags sticking from each one. The lids were secured with bungee cords. Zoe was certain the cans had been empty only a few days before.

She hesitated before getting out of the car, but the house was clearly deserted. There was no place for a car to be hidden from view.

With a self-deprecatory laugh, she swung open the door. Obviously, her brother Rob who lived nearby, or someone else in the family, had come down to clean out Ethan's refrigerator. While she was preoccupied with the speculative, trust Rob or his wife, Pauleen, to keep in mind the mundane details of what should be done.

Sure enough, a quick inspection revealed that the bags contained perishables and paper trash. Zoe refastened the bungee cords, protection against raccoons and the occasional bear. No doubt, Rob would be sending the refuse collectors down the access road any day now.

Just to still any further nagging fears, Zoe walked over to the garage, set on the uphill side of the house. There were no windows to peer into, but she checked the door. It was still securely locked. With a deep breath, she turned toward the house.

Inside, the air was no longer stale and empty. Someone had tidied up, thrown away the newspapers, washed the dirty dishes. In the kitchen, counters had been wiped clean. Zoe found her eye drawn to the coffeemaker. Given the state of the rest of the kitchen, she expected to find the pot washed clean. Ethan usually made a full pot in the morning, then drank all but one cup, leaving it to cool in reserve in case he needed the fortification later in the day.

As if he had brewed it only that morning before leaving, an extra cup stood in the pot. A sniff indicated it could pass for fresh. Between Tuesday and Sunday, Zoe expected to see mold of some kind growing on the liquid.

Blinking back sudden and unexpected tears, Zoe berated herself. Of course, Rob or Pauleen would have made the coffee while they were cleaning. Although they did not often drink coffee, Ethan was probably out of tea, so they'd settled for what they could find.

With a sob that startled her by its depth, Zoe reached for the countertop and hung on. The smell of the coffee caught in her throat and made it constrict. Tears that, until that moment, she had successfully sat on like a suitcase stuffed to overflowing, suddenly coursed down her face.

Although, in the midst of it, she had thought she would never be able to stop crying, eventually the tears began to dry up. Zoe's throat was raw, and her eyes burned, but the fear and anxiety she had so safely hoarded from exposure were gone. She splashed water on her face and squared her shoulders.

Before she could take another look around the kitchen to find the next landmine awaiting her, she hurried to the phone and dialed her friend Kip Chaney, who was, Zoe hoped, hanging out at home in the house up the hill behind her own. Although Zoe had called the number only a handful of times before, she was not surprised to find she knew it by heart, already.

"Kip, it's Zoe. Want to share a pizza and watch a basketball game?" she asked in a voice she did not recognize as her own.

"Are you okay, Zoe?"

"Fine. I'm at Ethan's house because I don't have cable at home. The high school basketball game from Tuesday is going to be shown at seven. It's important that I see it. Would you be interested in watching?"

Without hesitation, Kip answered, "Want me to pick the pizza up?"

"That sounds great." Kip held two part-time jobs, one as a bookkeeper and one as the on-site security guard at the house remodeling project currently underway on the property next to Zoe's. Zoe knew Kip's finances were shaky. "I already called for the pizza so it should be ready when you get there. Let me give you directions."

Pulling out napkins and glasses, Zoe dialed her brother's number. "Rob," she said, tucking the phone between shoulder and chin, "Ethan's house looks great."

"What do you mean?"

"Weren't you down here cleaning up?"

"Aw, Zoe, we haven't had a minute. First the rain, then the

snow . . . I've meant to get down there, but we've been so busy. The only break we had, a few days ago, we used it to visit Ethan in the hospital."

"Well then, who was here?"

"Maybe Eric. If Aunt Helen and Uncle Ed are staying there, he'd be sure to tidy up."

"They're staying at the motel near the hospital. Eric thought it would be easier on them."

Zoe imagined the shrug as Rob replied, "Well, maybe it was still him. You know how he likes to take care of things."

"Maybe," Zoe conceded. "But then again, maybe we've all been too preoccupied with Ethan to worry about his house."

"You think an unemployed cleaner broke in and went over the place in order to keep his skills sharp?"

"It's as good an explanation as any." Although Zoe kept her tone even and light, her lower lip found itself between her teeth. Cleaning Ethan's place was hardly a sinister move, but it was an unsettling one. Any one of her brothers or sisters might have thought of it, but none of them had a key. Except for Rob and her.

"Well, should I send the truck down when the guys come for pickup?"

As her lips began to say yes, Zoe reconsidered. "Not yet, Rob."

Maybe the police would be interested in examining those bags. They were potentially important. If some clue had been hidden among the perishables, she didn't want to throw it in the dump.

As she said good-bye to her brother, she tentatively dialed the county police, not sure just what she intended to report once she was connected. Jennifer Randolph was not working, and Zoe did not have her home number. She considered leaving a message for the FBI but could imagine the response it would get. There was no way she could phrase what had happened in Ethan's house without sounding upset about a phantom housecleaner. At best, the bags would be sent to the state crime lab. At worst, though, Zoe would be sternly warned to stay out of Ethan's house and the investigation.

With a frown, she put down the phone.

"This is my very first basketball game ever," Kip announced, tucking her long, gray-streaked hair behind her ears as she settled back on Ethan's couch. "Even when I was in high school, I was never interested. Mind you, show me a mainframe, and it was love. There were no PCs then, which gives you an idea how ancient I am."

"You're forty," Zoe said, reaching for a slice of pizza, happy to slip easily into banter with a friend in Ethan's home. It reminded her of the comfort she usually felt in the place. "When are you checking into that retirement home, anyway?"

"You don't strike me as the basketball type, either," Kip raised her eyebrows, inviting Zoe's response.

"What's the basketball type? I'll have you know I *played* basketball in high school."

"You're not tall enough!"

"I didn't say varsity basketball. I got together with a bunch of other kids, and we played for the fun of it."

Kip laughed. "Undermined your entire school system, I'll bet. I pretty much just kept to myself. I didn't even join the computer club. It was all boys, and I knew I wouldn't fit in there, either. It was a tough place for a geeky kid. All I was interested in was physics. It was the only subject that entranced me. When I thought about physics, nothing else mattered."

"You still think about physics?"

Kip sighed. "When I can. It doesn't take me soaring anymore,

though. I haven't been able to keep up with the latest develop-
ments in my field. I'm afraid to get the journals. I'm sure he'd
come up with a way to find me through the subscription lists. I
can't risk that again. And I don't dare get in touch with former
colleagues, even via e-mail. I'm afraid it's all passing me by now."

"I'd be glad to subscribe for you. Even under another name. All
the literature could come to my box."

With a sad smile, Kip shook her head. "Your name, or
whichever name you'd use, wouldn't be known to anyone else in
the field. That'd be a sure giveaway."

"Is your field really that small?"

"Afraid so."

"How about using my computer?"

"Oh, Zoe, I appreciate your wanting to help, but I just couldn't
risk it. Even if he couldn't find me, which I don't put past him,
he'd find a way to send me a message. And I don't want that,
either. No, it's best I stay away. I just wish there had been something else that interested me in school."

"Was it a good school?"

Zoe knew better than to ask where Kip had gone to school.
Years of deliberate obfuscation had rusted the hinges on the door
to Kip's personal information.

"Good? It had a reputation out to there! You've never heard of
the place, though, I'm sure," Kip said, attempting unsuccessfully to
recapture the lightheartedness in her tone. Then she added, "It was
upper class. Suburban. All the amenities. More than 85 percent of
all graduates went on to college. Was it like that at your school?"

"I don't know. With ten kids, my family skewed all of the statis-
tics. I think the West Virginia average is under 20 percent for high
school seniors going on to college. But every one of my siblings
attended college, one way or another."

Tilting her head as she wiped her mouth, Kip asked, "What

made your parents spur you all on? No education themselves?"

Zoe froze in midbite and removed her mouth from around the pizza. Quizzically, she asked, "What makes you think my parents had no education? They both graduated from college."

A look of confusion swept across Kip's face. "I guess . . . I thought you told me you were poor. I guess I just assumed deprivation. How did you come to grow up in Moody Hollow, West Virginia?"

"Poor by choice," Zoe said with an inward smile. Those three words had been her parents' mantra. "My mom came to coal country through VISTA, as a community activist. She met my dad, who was just back from the Peace Corps and looking for something meaningful to do with his life. Together, they thought they could make a difference. The importance of money was always dismissed. My parents treasured other things."

"Whoa! Idealists! And I thought I was out of place in P—" Kip's eyes clouded. She studied Zoe briefly, made her decision, sighed. "Pittsburgh. I went to school in Pittsburgh."

Zoe skipped over voicing the reassurance that Kip's secret was safe with her. "Not only idealists," she said. "Jewish, too. The double whammy."

"Kiss of death," Kip smiled warmly. "I heard your brother tell Shep Tuttle you were Jewish. Me, too."

"Yeah?"

They both smiled into their slices of pizza.

"Why did I have to find out from your brother? I've never heard you talk about being Jewish."

"I am the least religious person I know," Zoe confided. "Yet Judaism makes me who I am."

"I wish I'd had the religious education," Kip began, but interrupted herself to announce, "Look, the game is starting! What am I supposed to be looking for?"

"A young woman, fourteen, long brown hair, not real clean, a streak of bright red about an inch wide down the right side of her hair. Maybe wearing a leather jacket. And a tall, blond young man, probably seventeen. Floppy hair, very clean. Really broad shoulders. They should be sitting in the bleachers. Every time the crowd is panned, I want to try to find them."

"Together?"

"No. He should be sitting right behind her."

"I don't think your young couple was there," Kip said as the game wound down, after Zoe had filled her in on the details of Ren and Billy. "Although maybe they didn't get in the picture. The video crew was there to record the game, not the crowd, remember. Maybe they were there, and we just didn't spot them."

"The game's over. The cameras scanned the crowd several times. I think we would have at least seen that streak of red hair."

"Maybe she had it covered up."

Zoe clicked off the TV, shaking her head. "It looks as if someone's lying about being at that game. Why would Billy Johns lie about Ren being at the basketball game? Maybe he wasn't there himself?"

Kip sipped from her can of cola, playing devil's advocate with a finesse Zoe admired. "You say Ren's family has money. Maybe Ren paid Billy off. If he's not so well off, he's going to need quite a sum to go to a good college. Even if he gets a full scholarship, he's going to need books and stuff. Did you go to school on scholarship? Did you need spending money?"

Zoe laughed. "Did I need spending money?" During her undergraduate years, Zoe had worked summers in construction and during school terms for student health services. She had needed whatever money she could scrape together.

Zoe started thinking aloud. "How would Ren ever have met

Billy? Sure, she might know he's the quarterback of the football team, if she follows football at all, but he's a junior, and she's just a freshman. That's a huge gap in high school."

With her long fingers, Kip pounced on a mushroom that had slid off the pizza. As she popped it in her mouth, she speculated, "Maybe she's blackmailing him. Maybe she saw him do something he shouldn't have been doing. Maybe telling this lie about Ren is his payoff to her."

"What could she have seen? Billy playing baseball instead of football?"

Kip tilted her head. "Maybe the kid steals cars in his spare time."

Zoe paused, holding back the easy denial that had prepared to take off from her lips like a diver into a pool. "Maybe he sells drugs. Ren smokes marijuana. She has to get it somewhere."

This time it was Kip who retorted with amusement, "And she's his one sure sale every week, huh? So he lies for her to protect his client. Why do you find it necessary to blame the squeaky-clean kid? Hey, who won that basketball game, anyway?"

"I don't know."

The two women smiled at each other, and Zoe relaxed against the back of Ethan's couch.

Kip turned sideways toward Zoe, resting her knee on the cushion. "One question bothers me, aside from how Ren knows Billy, and why Billy lied for Ren: why didn't Ren choose someone who was actually at the game to lie for her?"

Slowly, Zoe nodded, the hint of a smile tracing its way across her features. "That's it, Kip! Ren didn't choose! She's sticking by her story that she was under the tree across the stream when the shootings took place. She didn't ask for anything. It's Billy Johns who claims he saw her at the basketball game. She never claimed she was there at all."

"But you told me Ren lies all the time."

Zoe blinked slowly. "Maybe Ren told the truth this time."

"But she gave you the wrong vehicle. That was a lie."

"Yeah. Maybe. Or maybe it was habit. One of the county cops told me Ren puts that truck at crime scenes regularly. Maybe this time, Ren really did see it. No one seems to have thought of that."

"Oh, Zoe, don't tell me they're going to put your picture in the dictionary under the entry for 'wild goose chase.' Surely the FBI would have checked out the guy."

"Ellis Anton is his name. He's Ren's cousin. Maybe that's who she saw with the gun across the stream. And I think you're giving the FBI a tad too much credit. If every cop they meet tells them Ellis Anton is a dead end, it's my bet they don't spend the resources to check him out."

"Yeah, and he could have been at Kennedy's assassination, had he been born then. Maybe he could have seen the burglars at the Watergate. Or, he could have been at Woodstock! I wish I'd been at Woodstock!"

Zoe affectionately patted Kip's shoulder. "Next time warp, we'll go together."

A simple mailbox with the name "Anton" painted on the side marked the turnoff from the road. Although it was graded and blacktopped, the lane to the house was no wider than the pot-holed track Zoe used as her driveway. Second-growth trees dominated the hillsides. Very little landscaping had been done.

Zoe drove around a curve, and the sight she encountered made her breath stick in her throat. The Anton house was perched on the top of a mountain, its back hanging precariously over the precipice. All angles and planes, it was composed as much of glass as wood, as much of open spaces as closed. Designed so that views in every direction could fill the eye from inside.

The lane twisted back into the trees before leading to a circular drive, where Zoe parked her old Chevy beside a late-model BMW.

The walkway to the house was native stone, laid down in an understated swirl that carried a person along to the front door. Massive chestnut panels, the grain so burnished it stood out almost as legibly as if it had been embossed, stopped Zoe a few feet away from the house.

She stood several seconds in admiration of the wood and the skill of the artisan who had seen and preserved it.

When she rang the bell, she heard no sound inside. Stained glass panels on either side of the door were evocative of raptors, although Zoe could not discern how it had been done, actual depictions of any birds at all not being part of the design.

There was so much to occupy the eye and mind that Zoe was unaware the door had opened until a man cleared his throat.

He was a young man, taller than Zoe by several inches, well-fed, and posture-perfect. Dark hair, short on the sides and longer on top, capped a round face that was still creased from sleep. He wore no shirt, so it was obvious he exercised regularly. Once he was certain he had Zoe's attention, he finished fastening the top button of his jeans.

Smiling inquisitively, he tilted his head. "Not selling Girl Scout Cookies, are you?"

"I'm sorry to bother you. I would have preferred calling first, but the number isn't listed. I'm Zoe Kergulin. Are you Ellis Anton?"

His fingers tapped his bare chest, playing it the way children pretend to make music on desktops that stand in for pianos. "That would be me. What can I do for you?"

"I'm an investigator, Mr. Anton. I'm looking into the police shootings last Tuesday. I'd like to ask you a few questions."

Shrewdly, he sized her up. "An investigator," he repeated. "Not the police or the FBI."

"No. The private variety."

He nodded slowly, as if all had suddenly been made clear, but he asked, "What makes you think I know anything about that shooting?"

"Someone placed your pickup at the scene."

A loud guffaw erupted from him, nearly doubling him over. When he straightened, he laughed again, briefly, until he could get it under control. "You've been talking to my cousin, Ren. Geez, Zoe, not even the local police give credence to anything she says. No one believes her. She thinks I committed every crime that's ever been reported, and then some. What's she think I did now? Shoot those two cops?"

Without waiting for an answer, he stepped back from the door. "You might as well come in. It's starting to rain again. My parents are away for a few days, so you'll have to excuse the mess. Would you like something to drink? I've got these power shakes that really rev you up. Not bad tasting, either."

"No, thanks."

If anything, the inside of the house was even more spectacular than the face it presented to the world. Natural wood gleamed on the floors, the walls, the furniture, and the ceilings. Even given the gray day, the light on the wood cast a shining glow.

The living room was extended by a deck that seemed to be suspended over the rest of the state.

"Go ahead," Ellis Anton shrugged. "That window and deck are going to hold your attention until you step over and have a look. I don't know why my parents built this place if they expected people to talk here. Their mouths open, as if they're going to say something, but the jaw simply drops and stays there."

"It is pretty impressive," Zoe said, turning as she took in the room. The place looked more like a modern museum than it did a house. She wondered how anyone could live there comfortably. Although, she reflected, people had probably thought the same of her comfortable Queen Anne in the days of its opulence.

He shrugged again. "It's home. My parents built it about ten years ago. It's been in all the magazines. Mom designed it. She's an architect. She says she wanted to build something the world would remember. Usually she does commercial buildings, but she put everything she had into this house. You should see my apartment and studio in the walk-out basement. She thought of everything."

"Your studio? Are you an artist?"

"Photographer. Not these vistas, either. I like detail. In close. Mostly I do portraits. You sure you don't want a protein shake?"

"I'm sure. Thanks."

While Ellis Anton disappeared into the back of the house, Zoe strolled from window to window, marveling at the panorama. A red-tailed hawk shrilled its wild cry from below her.

When he returned, Ellis Anton settled easily on one of the couches facing a maple coffee table. He sipped a chalky-looking liquid from his glass, raised a bare foot to the edge of the table, and tilted his head toward the couch opposite. "Please, have a seat. What is it I can do for you?"

As she sat on the surprisingly uncomfortable cushion, Zoe asked, "Did you know Rosalyn Fitzgerald?"

"She the dead cop?" At Zoe's nod, Ellis continued, "Nope. I didn't even know she lived so close to my aunt and Ren. Did Ren know? I'll bet it was a shocker to her, having a cop as a neighbor."

He laughed, then abruptly stifled the sound when Zoe did not join in.

"Do you know Ethan McKenna?"

"That's the sheriff, right? I've never talked to him, no. I think I might have voted for him once. How's that?"

"Why is it that Ren said she saw your truck at the scene of the shooting on Tuesday afternoon?"

He shook his head. "I have no idea."

"But she's apparently done it on a regular basis. Surely you've thought about it."

"I've thought about it, sure. But I still don't know. Maybe she's jealous of me. I got the money, the parents, the talent, the looks.

I'm not bragging, but I'm not falsely modest, either. Ren didn't get much on any of those scores, did she? Except the money. And her family's only got that because my dad's a generous brother. Basically, Ren's a loser in a family of losers."

Zoe found her chin rising of its own accord, as if attached to a helium balloon. The money, the parents, the talent, the looks. It was immediately apparent what was valued by the scion of the Anton family.

"How long has Ren been telling these stories about you?"

The contents of the glass slopped weakly over the rim as Ellis flung wide his hands. "I don't know. Ever since she could talk, I think. It's something I've learned to laugh at. She comes up with some whoppers. What else did Ren say about me?"

"What else were you expecting her to say?"

"I never know. It beats me where she gets these stories. Once she called 911 and told them I was giving out poison candy for Halloween. When the bank got robbed, she called the news hotline at some local TV station and turned me in for that. Whenever there's a report that someone's been robbed or kidnapped, Ren calls the police and identifies me as the culprit."

"It sounds as if she really has it in for you."

"The kid has some major problems. She needs help."

"And you don't remember how she got started?"

While shaking his head, Ellis took another sip of his drink. "It was about the time her parents were divorced. Maybe that had something to do with it. Maybe I was the nearest male relative and handily available when the time came for Ren to take all that anger out on someone."

He finished his shake, studying the bottom of the glass as if looking to interpret tea leaves. "I'm no psychologist, but that could be where it all started."

"Where is your truck now?"

"Down around back, in the garage. Why?"

Zoe shrugged. "Just wondering. Is that BMW out front yours?"

He spread his hands and grinned. "Can't expect me to recreate in my work vehicle, can you? Hey, are you working for my Aunt Lila? Is that who hired you?"

"No."

"Who are you working for, then?"

Levelly, Zoe answered, "Ethan McKenna's family. He's my cousin."

"Your cousin? Glad I didn't say anything bad about him!"

A sad smile crept across Ellis Anton's lips as he returned to the subject of his own cousin. "I really don't know why Ren is the way she is. Maybe it has something to do with us both being only children. Are you an only child, Zoe?"

"No."

"Well, like everything, it has its good points and its bad ones. Me, I think I got the good things. I like being the center of my parents' attention all the time. Even now, and I'm twenty-four. Ren, I think she's got the downside of being an only child. Anything bad she does is magnified because there are no other siblings to do their own bad things and share the wrath of her parents. And she's been doing bad for so long, she can't stop. I think she doesn't know how to. So she's caught in a cycle, repeating the same mistakes over and over again."

"So?" Willa asked over the rim of her coffee cup. She had arranged to meet Zoe for brunch at the Sinksville Ordinary after the interview. The place was a combined general store, motel office, and diner. "You're late. Is everything okay with Ethan?"

"Fine."

"So, what happened?"

"So," Zoe said, "thank you for the directions to the Anton house."

"The Anton estate, I think, babe. Overwhelming, huh? I did a human interest story on them last year. I didn't want to tell you the details beforehand and muck up your impressions."

"Tell me now." Zoe set aside the menu and crossed her arms in front of her on the table.

"Did you meet all of them?"

"Only Ellis, the son."

"Well, he's the most interesting, isn't he? And the one you wanted to talk to. Did he come on to you? Here, help me with this muffin, please. I had no idea they were this big!"

"No, thanks, I want a piece of apple pie. I know Ardell was making two big ones when I talked to her yesterday."

"Apple pie for breakfast?"

"For eating. Why are you asking if Ellis Anton came on to me?"

"Because what happened when I was there was so strange. His parents both left the room to get different things to show the photographer. The photographer tagged along with Lynn Anton. They were having a conversation about printmaking that I could not follow. So Ellis and I were shooting the breeze alone, not saying much of anything, just marking time. Or so I thought. He thought I was flirting with him."

"You?" Zoe feigned shock.

"Maybe I was, just a little. But he came right out and said, 'Ms. Fiore, I have to tell you before this goes any further, I'm not the least bit attracted to women.'

"I practically fell off my chair, Zoe! I was just passing time with the guy! I had no intention of dating him! He must be at least three or four years younger than I am!" Willa grinned to emphasize she had considerably lessened the distance between her age and Ellis Anton's.

"He didn't really come on to me," Zoe said, interrupting herself to stand in order to give Ruth Cook a proper hug hello. Ruth and her sister, Ardell, ran the Ordinary. The sisters were responsible, with a little help from Willa, for getting Zoe involved with the modern-day Underground Railroad. "How's that cousin of yours doing?" Ruth asked.

"Coming along."

"You tell me what you need, what Ardell and I can do for you."

"You're doing it, Ruth," Zoe said and hugged her again before resuming her seat.

"So?" Willa prompted. "He didn't really come on to you, but—?"

"But he had his shirt off—"

"For me, too!" Willa declared in amazement, her hand reaching across the table to touch Zoe's arm. "And he didn't so much fondle himself as just keep tabs."

"Yes." Zoe nodded. "He touched himself often. His chest, his stomach."

"He works out. That's obvious. He may not be attracted to women, but he sure wants us to notice him."

"Anyway, he insisted he knows nothing about the shooting. He claimed to be amazed that anyone had even listened to what Ren had to say."

"Did you believe him?"

"What's not to believe? There's no evidence that links him to the scene. Not yet, anyway."

As Ruth slid the plate of apple pie in front of Zoe, she smiled encouragingly. "Try it. Ardell says she used three different kinds of apples."

"Thanks, Ruth," Zoe replied.

Willa waited until they were alone again before leaning toward Zoe. "Listen, I have something to tell you."

Something in Willa's tone made Zoe freeze, fork poised before her mouth.

"Zoe, did you know that Rosalyn Fitzgerald's husband, Kirk, confided to a coworker that he suspected the sheriff was having an affair with his wife?"

"Yeah, right." In spite of her disbelieving tone, Zoe lowered the bite of pie untouched to her plate. Her mouth suddenly tasted of sawdust.

"It's true, Zoe. I hate to be the one to break it to you, but you had to be told. It's going to be front-page news in all the local papers. You're going to be hearing it on the radio and TV.

"It was around the end of December. Kirk Fitzgerald told this guy that his wife was working all kinds of strange hours. He didn't really believe she could be working that much. He suspected there was something else going on."

Making an expression of dismissal, Zoe said, "Just because he had suspicions doesn't make it so, Willa."

"Zoe, he showed up at the sheriff's department. Deputies remember him coming in. He wasn't happy. He wanted to talk to Ethan. Now, Chickie Ondean claims that Kirk Fitzgerald was put out about his wife missing some Christmas party at his office in Wheeling and wanted some clarification from Ethan about Rosalyn's schedule. Chickie didn't come out and say so, but he implied that maybe Kirk had already had one or two drinks more than he should have. Someone else told me that Ethan tried to usher Kirk to a more private spot, that he kind of put his arm around Kirk's shoulders, but Kirk shrugged him off.

"You know how the media are going to present that. Chickie's the only one who says Kirk came to talk about his wife's schedule, but who's going to buy that? I'm telling you as a friend, Zoe. I know it's upsetting, but the last thing I want is for you to hear it from a stranger and wonder why I didn't warn you."

"Either way, I'm going to be upset, Willa. And either way, I don't believe a word of it, except for what Chickie had to say."

"I don't know, Zoe. As early as last year, Rosalyn Fitzgerald's husband suspected there was something going on. And, apparently, Ethan never denied it in public."

"We're off the record here, right?"

It took a second longer than Zoe had hoped for, but Willa nodded.

Zoe continued, ticking off her points on her fingers, "Okay. If this story is true, it proves nothing about any alleged affair. Ethan had no need to deny what never happened. All your story shows is that Kirk Fitzgerald maybe talks when he shouldn't. That might be bad judgment, but it's no crime. And if it reinforces his status as prime suspect, I still don't see how he managed to get across the state and back in record-breaking speed."

"That will come out eventually, I'm sure. The state police and the FBI are working on it right now. They're checking charters and private flights . . . It's going to take a while, but they'll find out how he did it. The important thing is that not only did Kirk Fitzgerald suspect the affair, he even showed up at the sheriff's department to verify his suspicions. There are witnesses."

Zoe blinked. "When Ezra Cutcheon rides his tractor to the Bickle County Fairgrounds, and then stands on it in the middle of the field beside the highway and points out the paths of angels descending, is he cluing everyone in on some truth?"

"Zoe," Willa said exasperatedly, "other people already suspected the affair. Other people in the department. When Kirk Fitzgerald came by with fire in his eyes, that pretty much sewed it up for them. Besides, let's not forget that Ethan was practically sitting in Rosalyn's lap," Willa added sadly, as if regretting having to bring up the subject again.

"There's no proof, Willa."

The reporter threw up her hands. "Zoe, I'm trying to break the truth to you in a dosage that's easy to take. Don't you see, the affair explains everything! Rosalyn maybe did receive some special attention in her career. And she and Ethan carried on for a few months, at the end of which Kirk Fitzgerald had enough. He ambushed them in his own driveway."

With a clatter, Zoe's chair skittered behind her as she stood. She leaned in close to say, "Ren saw two people running down the front lawn just after the shooting. How do you explain that?"

"Ren? Oh, come on, Zoe! Is Ren the best you can do?"

"How can you make this fluff and nonsense the best *you* can do, Willa?"

Zoe fished blindly in her pocket for money. Coming up with only a five-dollar bill, she breathed heavily as she threw it on the table next to the pie she had not tasted.

"Zoe, I'm sorry. Give me a counterpoint, and you know I'll work it in."

The defiance had drained from Zoe in the face of her friend's obvious remorse, but the disappointment remained. She studied Willa's face for the briefest of moments.

"I'm sorry, too, Willa," she said. "I have nothing else to say." With that, Zoe lifted her chin and walked deliberately out into the fitting rain.

When he pressed the packet into her hand, Bob Farmer grabbed her palm for a moment. The sight of the janitor's grimy and calloused fingers on her skin was enough to make Ren want to scream.

Panicked, she forced herself to look up at him with a question on her face.

Farmer smiled. A nauseating gray colored his teeth.

Ren tried to smile back, wondering why he hadn't taken his hand off hers already.

"I hear tell you saw that shooting last week. Word's out you live over that way."

Ren shrugged noncommittally and slid her fingers over the packet in her palm as the weight of Farmer's hand slowly lifted from hers. As she quickly stowed the little packet inside her jacket, she said, "The cops caught me shoplifting. I had to tell them something to get them to let me go. So I said I saw everything that happened when those two got shot."

Her mouth was going dry, but Ren ignored it and forged on. She mixed a sneer with a shrug. "First, I thought about telling them it was aliens, but I figured they wouldn't buy that. So then I fingered my weird cousin, but they didn't really care for that story, either. So I made something up about a couple of foreign guys. I had 'em speaking Spanish and playing the radio really loud. I'll bet the cops are looking all over the county for them!"

"Yeah?" The janitor's eyes narrowed. Oh so casually, he snugged his hands into the pockets of his overalls. "Didn't they ask you how it was you recognized Spanish?"

Ren almost laughed out loud, the question was so obvious an attempt to catch her in a lie. "Hey, I take Spanish. First year. ¿Cómo está usted? Besides, my mother had a maid from Honduras once. I know what Spanish sounds like."

"Why'd you say *two* guys?"

"Huh?" Ren felt her heart suddenly bang against her chest. That question she had not anticipated.

"Why'd you say two guys? Everyone else says one."

Ren shrugged. "Gee, I don't know. I guess it was the first thing that popped into my head. Maybe I saw it on a video. Half the time, I never know what I'm going to say until the words are already out of my mouth."

Farmer smiled, gray teeth slowly looming larger and larger as his lips parted. The image reminded Ren of a horror-movie monster. Without being aware of doing so, Ren's hand clutched at a fistful of sweatshirt over her stomach.

The janitor said, "Where were you, really?"

"Who the hell knows?" Ren heard the shaky laugh come from her throat. It was pathetic. "I guess I was getting high somewhere. That's what I usually do when I leave this place. I hate being here, and I hate being home."

"Poor little girl's got nowhere to go. Lucky you got me to take you elsewhere. What would you do without me, little girl?"

Ren let her eye wander down the darkened, empty hallway. Tapping that part of the jacket that covered the hidden pocket inside, she deliberately turned the conversation away from herself. "When do you think you can score more of the GHB?"

"You that anxious to get laid?" He laughed uproariously at his own joke, knowing only that the colorless liquid he had sold to Ren was one of a group of date-rape drugs. Wiping his eyes with the palm of a stained hand while individual guffaws continued to putter from his lips, Farmer added, "Maybe next week. Things are hot right now. Maybe not until the following week. I'll let you know. Just keep the money handy. I've had lots of requests for the stuff. Price might be going up."

The laughter stopped, and the attempted smile turned downward as the janitor lowered his voice. "Don't you be talking to the cops at all. You'd be amazed at how easy it is to overdose on anything, even the crap you smoke, if it's laced with the right stuff. You understand me, little girl?"

Ren hated the tone in Farmer's voice even as she trembled before it. That made her despise herself even more. Although her lower lip threatened to quiver, Ren balled up her left hand and dug her nails into her palm at the same time she stepped closer to Farmer.

"Don't you be talking to the cops, either!" she growled, almost losing control of her voice. It was a stupid thing to say, she knew, but maybe Bob Farmer was too much of an idiot to realize it.

With that, Ren touched the pocket that held the marijuana, then pivoted away from the custodian and walked down the empty hall, willing herself not to look back. She straightened her shoulders, her back rigid, but on her face was a terrified wince.

Almost every day after school, during the weeks when there was no football practice, Billy Johns ran. If the track was dry, he ran outside, around the football stadium. When it was wet, he ran inside, sometimes around the gym and sometimes through the halls and up and down the stairs. Wherever he ran, he never went alone. Friends and teammates worked out with him.

For Ren, who watched more times than not, Billy ran far out in front of the others, with a golden glow surrounding him, inside or out. She had never known anyone so handsome or so charming.

As always, she settled herself on the bleachers near his backpack. As always, she noted the order with which his socks were folded into his shoes. Billy Johns was no slob. He took his time with his things.

That he changed into special shoes and clean socks for running had made Ren's initial approach a lot easier.

Before he had known who she was, back when she'd been just another girl who drooled after the hotshot quarterback, Ren had eavesdropped as he changed out of his track shoes.

"It's called GHB," he'd told his buddy. "It stands for gamma hydroxybutyrate acid. I can't tell you how long it took me to sound out that word!"

Although she had deliberately not looked, Ren knew he had flashed his teeth in the way that made her heart melt.

"It builds muscle mass," Billy had continued. "It sounded great in the article I read on the Internet, but you can't just pick it up at the health food store anymore. I wish I knew how to get my hands on some!"

After that, it was easy for Ren to introduce herself to Billy. As soon as she scored the GHB the first time, she ran to the stadium. Hurriedly scribbling a note to wrap around the little packet, Ren slipped onto the bleacher next to Billy Johns' backpack. There, under the pretext of dropping her math book, she quickly slid the package under the sock in his left shoe.

Then, after she judged sufficient time had passed, she collected her things and went to the end of the bleachers, near the trash can, where she had written that Billy could see her so he would know the note wasn't bogus and the GHB was for real.

She didn't want Billy to pay her. She only wanted to see him turn the glow of his smile on her. And, after she had been supplying him for a while, she dared to ask him to meet her behind the library, where kids made out on summer evenings.

He had parked his car, leaving the engine running. Although the windows were tinted and Ren couldn't see inside, she knew his girlfriend was in there.

Ren had half-expected as much, and she was all set to tell Billy Johns that she couldn't get him any more of the drug, but he had actually put his hands on her shoulders and almost pulled her to him. The thought flashed through her mind that he might have kissed her, if only his girlfriend hadn't been sitting just around the corner.

"Ren." His lips had pronounced her name. "You're the best!"

And he'd squeezed her upper arms, pressure she could feel again whenever she closed her eyes and thought about him. "I'd never be such a good quarterback without your help!"

She'd forced open her eyes so she could savor Billy Johns up close.

"If I can ever do anything for you, Ren, anything at all . . ."

And he might have kissed her on the forehead. She wasn't sure, and it wasn't the kind of thing she could ever ask him to clarify for her. She had closed her eyes in the rush of it all, and something had brushed her face. Part of her fantasy was imagining him kissing her as only the beginning of their meeting. It took off from there.

She had handed him the little packet, although she did not remember that part, and he had sprinted back to his car, sliding behind the wheel with a grace that made Ren sigh.

She cried then, although sorrow had nothing to do with her tears. Sobs of joy, so strong Ren thought her heart might not be able to handle the strange feeling, flung themselves against the red brick building. In her heart, Ren danced across the parking lot. Billy Johns liked her. The handsome star quarterback was her friend!

As she walked out of the stadium, replaying that wonderful scene in her mind, Ren never even noticed the silver Jaguar parked in the corner of the school lot, never saw the man behind the wheel fixing his eyes on her.

Ren hugged her books and skimmed across the parking lot, a secret smile on her face.

Despite knowing that Ethan's office had been taken over by Libby Gordon, Zoe was still dismayed to find the door closed. She sized it up, as if measuring the strength of an opponent, before knocking.

"Come," commanded the local representative of the FBI.

As she turned the knob and walked into once-familiar territory, now occupied by what she could not help thinking of as an invading army, Zoe saw Libby Gordon behind Ethan's desk and Andrew Prescott in the seat that might as well have had Zoe's flag planted on it. That chair was where she always sat—hunkered down and attentive or splayed and relaxed—when she was in Ethan's office. The boxes once piled on it had been moved to the floor.

Chickie Ondean sat woodenly on the worn couch. He did not meet Zoe's eye as she gave a general greeting.

"Did you have a chance to watch the videotape of that basketball game?" Zoe asked before her hand even left the doorknob. It occurred to her that she was uncomfortable with the thought of closing the door behind her, as if doing so kept Ethan out.

"I know you mean well, Ms. Kergulin," Agent Gordon said, her lips thin, "but I think it would be best if you stayed clear of this investigation. You're too close to it."

"If you think my relationship to Ethan McKenna is clouding my judgment, then just look at the videotape. It's pretty obvious that neither of those kids is in the bleachers."

Libby Gordon carefully laid down the pen she'd been holding. There was no noise as it made contact with the blotter. "Ms. Kergulin, I have no time for videotapes. An arrest has been made in the case. We have more important details to concentrate on. I think you should let the professionals handle this one."

Zoe stared at the woman. "Who's been arrested?"

Exasperatedly, Libby Gordon said, "Ms. Kergulin!"

Andrew Prescott shifted in Zoe's chair. Grimly but not unkindly, he said, "From what I understand, you're accusing the star athlete in this town of telling tales about the star liar. Zoe, maybe that videotape just didn't show everyone who saw the game. Maybe you're letting your emotions run away with your imagination."

"Forget the videotape, then. If you go only on what Ren Bertram and Billy Johns have told you, then you know that one of them is lying."

It sounded weak as she spoke the words, but Zoe almost felt compelled to repeat the statement.

"Maybe neither of them is lying," Libby Gordon said, squaring her shoulders, although her glance did no more than graze Zoe. "You know, people often have different interpretations of the same events. It could be that Johns thinks he saw Bertram at the game. Maybe she was there; maybe she wasn't. But that's not the point, don't you see? What we're concentrating on is who did the shooting.

"I have received calls about you from Ren Bertram's mother and from the family's attorney. As well as from Ellis Anton and his attorney. And I hear you want the crime lab to go through bags of Sheriff McKenna's trash. This investigation is taking up not only my days but my nights, too. There is precious little time as it is. The last thing I need is for anyone to start messing around where she doesn't belong. I know you mean well, Ms. Kergulin, but I must ask you to back off or risk being charged with obstruction of justice. And that's just for starters."

Although her mouth had gone dry, Zoe straightened her own shoulders. In the same calm voice she would once have used with an irate suspect, she said, feeling her tongue catch on her teeth, "I'm interested in only one thing, and it's the same thing that's guided me since Rosalyn Fitzgerald and Ethan were shot. I want to know who did it."

"Fitzgerald's husband has been arrested, Zoe," Andrew Prescott said quietly, his eyes on the edge of the desk.

"If Rosalyn's husband shot her and Ethan, then what happened to the spent shells? Have you found the gun he allegedly used? Why did he fire from ambush? Why not walk right up to the car? Why not do it in the house, for that matter? Why risk being observed by a witness?

"And then there's the really big question. How did he manage to get across the state and back in record time? Without leaving a trail?"

Although Libby Gordon breathed audibly for several seconds, a patronizingly tight smile struggled to hang onto her lips. "Nothing of what you say is relevant to our investigation," she said, the only one of the three law officers in the room to steadily meet Zoe's gaze.

"I understand you are used to a certain amount of leeway, used to coming and going from this building, used to sticking your nose into police business. Perhaps Sheriff McKenna made an error in judgment on that score, sharing information he had no right to share. I assure you, I have no intention of making the same mistake.

"I don't want to see you in this office or this station again, Ms. Kergulin, unless it's in a holding cell. Do you understand?"

By the time Zoe strolled casually into the hospital, it looked to any observer like nothing in particular occupied her thoughts.

But the appalling scene in Ethan's office played out, over and over again. Later, she would try to figure out how she could have handled things differently. For the time being, though, all she could do was hear the words repeated like a tape on an endless loop.

Early that morning, Ethan had been moved to a private room. Eric had called to report that his brother was comfortable, and security was in place. Zoe calmly made her way through the lobby, heading for the stairway beside the elevator. She pulled open the door and stepped in.

Once the door closed behind her, she flattened herself against the wall, furiously blinked back tears, and reached around her right side, groping for the comforting grip of a pistol that wasn't there. After her best friend's death, Zoe had intended never again to hold a weapon. Now, she would have given anything to have one in her grasp.

Ethan had two handguns and ammunition locked securely in a box in his house. She knew where they were, and she knew where he kept the key. It had taken a supreme act of will to direct her car toward the hospital and not to Ethan's house as she left the scene in his office.

It comforted her to know she could swing by and take one of those guns any time she desired. Such thinking was also the source of a hollow of disappointment that was settling in her chest, but Zoe chose to believe that the feeling arose from the way she had walked out of Ethan's office without uttering another word, leaving his door wide open behind her.

Subdued voices drifted down the hallway from the nurses' station, announcements from televisions washed over Zoe as she passed open doorways. In the distance, a thready, elderly voice moaned indistinctly.

Despite the struggles waged in the Intensive Care Unit, Zoe preferred the constant directed bustle that went on there to the more selective attention given to patients on the floors. In I.C.U., Ethan had more layers of protection between himself and the outside world. That was gone from the hospital at large, where anyone with a gun could walk in and try to finish what she or he had begun.

Zoe nodded to the lone security guard from the private firm Eric had employed. She dug in her pocket for her I.D., and even though the guard was one she recognized, he scrutinized her photo and her face before allowing her entrance.

Ethan's brother sat on the wide windowsill, hunched over an open folder in a briefcase. His face rose toward Zoe as she entered, and he grimly waved a halfhearted welcome.

Ethan's skin was more waxen than white. Although bruised-looking, his eyes were open, and they softened at the sight of her.

Finding herself at his side, his hand in hers, Zoe leaned over to kiss Ethan's forehead. It was hot and papery.

"Infection," Eric supplied. "The doctor was just in. She gave him something. With luck, whatever this is will respond quickly to treatment."

"How are you doing, Ethan?" Zoe asked. In response, he closed his eyes and tightened his fingers around hers.

Gently taking his hand between both of hers, Zoe nodded. This complication was no more than a detour. The fear she dared not face, that the Ethan she knew had been shattered by bullet fragments and smashed irretrievably against the hard confines of his skull, could crawl back to its dark hiding place. "Just a temporary setback. When you're out of here, Ethan—"

The arrival of two of the technical staff mercifully interrupted Zoe, who had no idea what she had intended saying to her cousin to complete her sentence.

She and Eric allowed themselves to be ushered out into the hall, where they walked toward a window. Rain spattered explosively against the glass. Zoe leaned against it to feel the coolness on her forehead. Only then did they begin to talk in low voices.

"I had to take my mother and father down to the cafeteria," Eric said with an ironic half-smile. He had always been considered the more handsome of the two boys, although Zoe could never see it. His dark eyes were too quick to judge, and his full mouth never far from a pout or a sneer. Now that he had come through for his brother in this crisis, Zoe knew she would have to reassess his character. "Mom couldn't stop crying, and Dad kept asking her if maybe they shouldn't call a priest in. Just what Ethan needs, huh?"

"Have you seen or heard any news?" Zoe asked, straightening her shoulders, although it meant leaving behind the wonderfully cold kiss of glass against her skin.

"No, only the flood warnings everyone's talking about. What's up?"

"Rosalyn Fitzgerald's husband has been arrested. Even though he was across the state when the shootings occurred. Everyone seems so eager to swallow the idea that he was avenging himself against his wife and the man who broke up his marriage. The real shooter is going to get clean away."

"Isn't the FBI in charge of the investigation? How could they allow the wrong person to be arrested?"

Zoe shrugged tiredly. "Wishing makes it so?"

"I'm going to have to make a statement on behalf of the family. Is everyone still staying at your house? I'll make sure I talk to them all, and then I'll release something to the media. Is that okay with you?" Eric asked perfunctorily. Zoe could see that he was already composing the statement in his head. He would use his court-room voice, enunciate clearly, and project to the back of the room.

"Whatever you want to say, Eric." Zoe wanted nothing to do with press statements. "Did you get anything more from the security firm about anyone trying to get in to see Ethan? Or even just calling about his condition?"

"Yes, I did. They faxed me a copy. I've got it right here." He pulled the neatly folded paper from an inside pocket. Opening it as he handed it to Zoe, he pointed out, "Of course, the county cops call regularly. A few of them have tried to see Ethan, but we've strictly limited visitors to family only."

Zoe quickly looked down the list. In each case, there were names associated with each attempt to visit Ethan. With one exception.

On two occasions, a man the security guards had described as a tall African-American with salt-and-pepper hair, well-dressed, and walking with a slight limp had attempted to get past the door that served as a checkpoint. Each time, upon being asked to provide identification, the man had left without further confrontation, except to enquire at a nurses' station about Ethan's condition. No information had been given to him.

"Is he with the media, do you think?"

Eric shrugged. "Other reporters have tried to use their credentials to get in. Except for one, who wore scrubs and thought he could sneak in without a hospital I.D. badge."

Zoe tapped the page by the description of the unknown man. "If he's not with the media, then who is he?"

"You're thinking he could be out to cause harm?"

"There's no mention that he threatened anyone, that he might have had a weapon. I don't know, Eric. I'm convinced Kirk Fitzgerald couldn't physically have done the shooting. Even if he contracted with a killer, that killer's still walking free. And if it was someone else, that widens the possibilities all the more." Zoe's exhalation was audible. "I'm just glad you've hired that security firm. It's the only protection Ethan has right now."

"Is there anything I can do to help you, Zoe? With all this digging around you're doing, maybe you should be armed."

A laugh spurted out before Zoe could stop it. It wasn't so much relief as the exposing of her darkest thoughts to the light, where they had to shrivel like vampires in the sun. The space at her waist that should have been covered by a holster, that should have supported the comforting weight of a handgun, still felt empty. But Zoe's hand no longer ached for the deadly weapon. Other possibilities for her grasp were opening up.

She threw her arms around Eric, startling him. "Thank you, Eric."

"For what?"

"For helping me get back on track."

"You did that yourself, if you were ever off track."

For the first time, Zoe saw Ethan in her cousin's face. With renewed determination, she told him, "I asked the investigating team to go over Ethan's garbage. Someone went through Ethan's kitchen and dumped the perishables in the cans outside. I thought it might have been Rob or Pauleen, but it wasn't. Maybe there was something in the house that would point a finger toward the shooter. Maybe it was more than someone could safely carry away, so they ended up hiding it in the trash. It's been so cold, I figured it would keep until the police lab could examine the contents of those garbage bags, but it's a task the local FBI agent in charge doesn't want to assume. I'm going to contact some old friends at the Justice Department. Someone should be able to pull some strings to help me get the contents of those bags analyzed. Maybe they can recover prints, if nothing else. And someone should be going through the crime scene again. I think they've missed clues in the rush to arrest Kirk Fitzgerald."

"You still keep in touch with those people? They didn't exactly rush to stand up for you when you needed them."

A smile of amazement lit Zoe from the inside. What the heck was Ethan doing in his brother's body?

When she had shot and killed Paul Martin, a split second after the man had murdered his estranged wife, Zoe's best friend, her immediate supervisor had distanced himself from the situation, claiming that the exchange of shots had been a personal matter between two people who happened to be Justice Department employees. No one wanted to claim foresight for what the volatile Paul Martin might have been capable of doing. That would have implied responsibility.

The ensuing investigation had fully cleared Zoe of any wrongdoing, but she had felt forsaken enough during the process to never want to see the place again. At sea personally and professionally, she had fled to the closest thing she had to home: Ethan in West Virginia.

"There are a few people I've kept in touch with," Zoe said, and added, "Maybe they can analyze a videotape for me, too."

She had taped the basketball game on Ethan's VCR. Sometime that day or the next, Zoe knew she'd have to get back to Ethan's place and retrieve the tape.

"If there's any help you need—financial, legal, or otherwise—

you let me know."

Squeezing Eric's arm, Zoe gave him another quick hug. "If you want to handle the media, that's more than enough for me. And if that man shows up again, trying to see Ethan, maybe someone could give me a call."

The high speed of the windshield wipers barely handled the volume of rain sweeping across the glass. All remaining caches of snow had melted, and deep puddles of water lurked in the shadows, like muggers looking for a score. In one deceptively low-lying section of asphalt, Zoe's old Chevy hydroplaned abruptly into the lane of oncoming traffic.

She fought the wheel and the wind to return to her lane, managing the maneuver just as a semi splashed by. With a whistle of relief, Zoe raised her shoulder to wipe away the film of sweat that had suddenly popped out on her face.

The defrost barely held its own. Zoe rolled down the window just enough to make a difference on the inside of the windshield, but the gale strong-armed its way into the car, too, soaking her left side and freezing her face.

By the time she reached the tiny village of Beverage, the nearest mailing address to her rural home, Zoe felt like a sailor who suddenly spots land after months on the sea.

The rain was still heavy, but it had lessened enough that the wipers had no trouble keeping up with it. Dark clouds, which had turned afternoon to night, suddenly showed cracks of light leaking across the sky.

Rolling up the window, Zoe breathed deeply. One hand at a time, she flexed her sore fingers before returning them to the wheel.

As she neared DeSoto's, the lone service station in the little town, she checked her gas gauge. In the split second between shifting her foot from the brake back to the gas, Zoe noticed someone in a yellow slicker standing near DeSoto's sign, waving to her.

With a quick turn of the wheel, she pulled into the station.

Her friend Kip peeked from the depths of the slicker's hood, and Zoe motioned her to the passenger side, leaning over as she did so to unlock that door. Kip worked two days a week at the station, keeping the books and lending a hand pumping gas when the place got busy.

"I'm going to soak your car!" Kip said, hesitating.

"Just get in!" Zoe ordered, even as she slid the dashboard lever to a spot midway between heat and defrost. Warm air immediately hit the lower part of her legs. "Are you okay? What's going on?"

Jack LaSalle, the mechanic who owned the station and kept her old car on the road, waved to Zoe from the lighted office. She returned the gesture before shifting her eyes back to Kip.

"I called your house and left a message with your brother David. He said you were probably at the hospital, so I knew you'd be passing by this way. I've been keeping a lookout for you."

Zoe said nothing, her face solemn, knowing whatever Kip was prefacing had to be important if she'd stood out in the storm waiting to flag down her friend.

"Is Ethan doing okay?"

"He's coming along," Zoe croaked, surprised to find her throat tight.

"Good. Listen, Zoe, there was a guy who stopped here. He was looking for you. He had your address—well, the old one with just the route and box number. He wanted to know how he could find your house. He said he was a friend. I hope I didn't do the wrong thing, but when Jack glanced at me, I took it for a warning, and I shook my head. Then Jack pulled his dumb hick act, and I did pretty much the same. I don't know what the man wants. Maybe he's a reporter. Maybe he really is a friend, but I thought, if you expected him, you would have given him directions."

Zoe's stomach dropped. "What did he look like?"

"Handsome. Maybe forty-five or so. Dark hair speckled with gray. Oh, and he walked with a limp. When he first got out of his car and came into the station, I really noticed the limp, but after he'd been on his feet for a few minutes, it wasn't so evident."

"African-American?"

Kip had to think about it. "Yes. And guess what he was driving? Jack said he'd never seen one in Beverage before."

"A silver Jaguar."

"You know this guy?" Kip turned an amazed expression in Zoe's direction.

"No. Did you warn David about him?"

"Well, I told David he was looking for you, and I told him he was driving the Jag. If that's warning, then I guess I did."

"Thanks, Kip. Was there anything else about him that stood out?"

Kip breathed hard and looked at the condensation creeping across the side window before she admitted, "Jack says he was carrying a gun. I didn't see it, but Jack said he noticed it right off. I saw his suit coat flap in the storm, because he wasn't wearing a jacket or even carrying an umbrella, and I know I didn't see any gun. But Jack is positive. Who is he, Zoe?"

"I don't know, Kip."

"You be careful, okay? Maybe—" Kip stopped herself from saying more.

Although Zoe had never gone into the details about Karen's death, she strongly suspected Kip had asked elsewhere and knew the entire story. Kip certainly knew that Zoe carried no weapon.

Zoe smiled at her friend with what she hoped was reassurance.

"We'll be fine. Can you imagine anyone in a Jaguar trying to get down my driveway? Even in good weather?" Inside, she was shaking. How could she protect herself, let alone Ethan and the rest of her family, from anyone determined to use a handgun?

The whuff of the phone book slamming closed coincided with Zoe's sigh. She had called every motel, inn, and bed and breakfast in Bickle County. Not one of them had a guest who drove a Jaguar.

"How about some coffee, Zoe?" her sister Rory asked, knocking on the office door as she opened it. Alongside her peered Cherry Pie, Zoe's sweet brown tabby. Smiling at the cat like a coconspirator, Rory displayed her bounty. "I brought some cookies, too."

As she leaned back in her chair, Zoe sighed again. "Come on in, you two."

"Any luck?" Rory boosted herself onto the table and bit into a cookie she had grabbed from the plate.

"None. Where would a stranger stay around here? The university only rents out dorm space in the summer."

"How about campgrounds?"

"I'm betting a guy in a suit and driving a Jaguar isn't camping out, but I wouldn't put it past him. Maybe I'll try those next."

Rory shrugged. "Aren't there still a couple of rooming houses near the university? They were seedy long ago, but if I wanted to hide out, I might think of going there."

Zoe wearily let her head fall in the direction of one shoulder as she surveyed her sister. "Anything's possible."

"While you were gone, during the storm, we had a visit from that sheriff from Feller County. He thought the driveway was just about impassable, but he said he was determined to get down here and make sure we were all okay. Geez, the guy drives one of those suburban assault vehicles. Like it was a hardship to dodge pot-holes in four-wheel drive! Anyway, he said to tell you he dropped by. He was going to visit the FBI next, to see how the investigation is going."

"They'll probably love him there," Zoe said, sipping from the wonderfully aromatic coffee one of her siblings had brought. "Especially Andrew Prescott."

Suddenly, Zoe straightened and banged the coffee mug on the desk. The weight of fatigue slid from her body.

"What?" Rory demanded.

"I'm going to be drummed out of the spook business! Rory, I limited my search to Bickle County. This guy could be staying in Feller County. Or even farther out. It's time I widened things."

Once again, she pulled the phone toward her. Cherry Pie jumped up on the desk and kneaded, purring, in a cat bed Zoe had placed there, close to her but away from the action when she talked on the phone or used the computer.

Rory slipped from the room as Zoe flipped through her directory.

While stroking Cherry Pie, Zoe punched in the phone number she'd found. Shep Tuttle came on the line as soon as he learned who was calling.

"Miss Zoe! I was out your way earlier today. So sorry I missed you! What can I do for you?"

"Sheriff Tuttle, I'm glad to have found you in."

"Oh, Miss Zoe, we've had some downed trees and some power outages. Flooding, too. You know I'm on the job in any emergency. I hope you're not calling to tell me you've got that river coming in your front door."

"No, Sheriff, that river is close, but it's several hundred feet down the mountainside. It would take quite a bit of rain and snow to bring it up to my front door. I am calling for a favor, though. Sheriff, I wonder if you've encountered that man you told me about, the one driving the sports car?"

"Black guy. I hear he walks with a limp. I've had my deputies keeping an eye out for him, but we haven't found him yet. Have you seen him, Miss Zoe?"

"No, Sheriff, and please call me Zoe. I've called all the motels and bed and breakfasts in Bickle County to see if they have a guest driving a silver Jaguar, but I've come up empty. I wonder if you could have someone fax me the motel pages of the Feller County phone book?"

"Fax you? Heck, I'll do better than that. I'll have my deputies make the calls themselves. Clerks will be more apt to answer a genuine deputy sheriff. I'll get them started on those calls right away. And I'll certainly let you know, once we find the guy."

It wasn't what she'd wanted, but Zoe was willing to settle for it. "Thanks, Sheriff."

"Say," he asked slyly, as if the thought had been in his head all along, but he was only now producing it, pretending the idea had just occurred to him, "are you and my buddy Mr. Prescott seeing each other socially? He's a heck of a guy, Miss Zoe, and I'd sure like to see him settled."

"Well, good luck to you, Sheriff." Zoe ignored his question.

"Now, don't you write him off. He's had some bad luck lately, what with his sting being interrupted and all, but he's going to make his bust. You wait and see. Why, are you aware that he has the record for participating in the most drug arrests in the shortest amount of time in various locales around this state?

"We had a narc here about a year ago who went and got himself killed. Mr. Prescott, though, he's a lot more careful. I'll tell you, Miss Zoe, he is one quick thinker, just like you. Why, that day Sheriff McKenna was shot nearby, we had a drug bust all set up at that very same Pumpkin Cave exit off the interstate. Mr. Prescott, he didn't have a radio on him, just in case the real dealers got antsy and searched him. So he had no way of knowing what was going on—"

"Excuse me, Sheriff," Zoe interrupted. "Your drug bust was out near where Ethan and Deputy Fitzgerald were shot? Who else knew about that sting, Sheriff?"

"Oh, Miss Zoe, I'm sure none of our team leaked that kind of information, if that's what you're thinking. Besides, we weren't really anywhere close to the scene of the shootings. It was an unfortunate coincidence, that's all."

"Did Ethan know about your sting operation?"

There was a pause while Shep Tuttle considered. "He knew we were involved in a sting. Hell, we worked with a liaison from his department. I really can't say if he knew the particulars."

"Who was the liaison from Bickle County?"

"Miss Zoe, I'm not sure I should be sharing that kind of information with you."

"Please, Sheriff. It might lead us to who did the shooting."

"I'm a pushover; I swear I am. It's Kendall Ondean, Chickie's son. Now, surely you know what a good cop he is."

It was true. Kendall had earned medals in the military police, he'd scored high on his civil service exam, and despite—or maybe because of—his innocent country-boy good looks, he was a very effective officer. Zoe knew Ethan thought highly of him.

She lowered her head to touch Cherry Pie's soft fur. In response, he purred. It was some consolation for the frustration of the road-blocks she seemed to keep hitting.

"I sure want to thank you for all your help, Sheriff Tuttle. I know you've been busy with everything the weather's throwing at you. And I'll look forward to hearing if your deputies find that man driving the Jaguar."

"My pleasure, Miss Zoe."

Just as she was about to hang up the phone, Zoe straightened as another thought occurred to her. She knew she was probably straying far afield of her own investigation, but she asked anyway. "Sheriff, I wonder if you could tell me just where that sting was supposed to take place in Pumpkin Cave?"

"Well, I don't see why I can't tell you. I know in meetings we've mentioned finding another place. No one wants to go back out that way. It was an abandoned farm. The state police did it up real nice for us so you couldn't even tell where the microphones or hiding places were."

Halfway between her mouth and the table, Zoe stopped the progress of the coffee cup. With a lurch and a slop of warm liquid, she set the mug on the desk, unaware of anything except the need to get a pen in her hand and paper in front of her.

"Can you give me directions to that farm, Sheriff?" She was remembering the wrong turn she and Willa had made the first time she drove out there, the abandoned farm they came across. Maybe it meant nothing, but her hand was shaking.

"Oh, Miss Zoe, I'd have to look them up. I always had one of my team drive up there, you know, and when you don't drive, you just don't pay attention. Now, the first time we went up there to check the place over, I did jot down a few notes so the rest of the team would be able to find the place."

"Who suggested it as the meeting place?"

"I don't really remember, Miss Zoe. We were discussing possible sites, and that one was decided upon. Maybe it was the state police. Maybe it was the bad guys."

"Sheriff, could you fax me those directions?"

"Well, I certainly could, Miss Zoe. I'll have one of the clerical staff do it first thing in the morning."

Zoe flipped off the light and peeked out through the slats covering the windows. She had shut the blinds in the round room that served as her office. There were so many windows that she had felt vulnerable and on display, despite the fact that the house sat a mile off the road, close to no neighbors. She could see nothing moving in the darkness.

Even knowing where the boulders jutted and the dips in the road were, Zoe had felt her car hit bottom a couple of times on her drive in. No one else, even a crazed killer with her name at the top of his hit list, would make it down her drive or through the intervening forest in the storm that still raged outside.

"I'd sure appreciate it if you could fax those instructions now, Sheriff," Zoe said, letting the slat drop back into place. "Let me give you the number."

"You can give me the number, Miss Zoe," Shep Tuttle gave a short laugh. "But I'm going to have to confess to you that I've never figured out copy machines, let alone faxes. I let my secretary do all that stuff."

"As soon as you can get them to me, then, Sheriff. I'll be waiting. And thanks for all your help."

"That's what I'm here for, Miss Zoe. I only wish you were a resident of Feller County so I'd have your vote in the next election."

Zoe's smile turned sickly, glad she lived in a time when cameras on phones were not commonplace. She thanked the man again and assured him she'd let him know if she turned up anything.

After replacing the phone in its cradle, Zoe rubbed her hands over her face. In truth, ready as she was to rush back into the storm, it was a relief to remain home. She'd been getting by on very little sleep and comfort foods. It would do her good to sit down for dinner at her own table, surrounded by the brothers and sisters she saw all too infrequently.

Sleep had come late, but that didn't stop Zoe from springing out of bed in the middle of the night. All four of her cats had huddled against her in the drafty darkness, and she had finally allowed herself to relax. With that surrender to unconsciousness had floated up, like a balloon through clouds, an answer she had been puzzling over.

The clock read 3:37 when Zoe whispered lovingly to the cats and settled the blankets around them on the bed. She slipped into jeans, transferred her essentials into the pockets, found a sweater —although in the dark she had no idea which sweater it was or what color it might be—and pulled it over her head.

Carrying her shoes and socks, she tiptoed downstairs to avoid waking her relatives. Aside from the usual creaking and groaning of the old house, the wind was all Zoe heard. For the moment, at least, it sounded as if the rain had stopped.

In the front hall, Zoe put on her socks and shoes before slipping into her jacket. She had her hand on the doorknob when she thought to go down the long hall to the kitchen, which necessitated stepping out of her shoes. On the back of a sheet of paper her sister Miriam had used for explaining in nauseating detail just what made a drain in a shoulder wound necessary, Zoe wrote a note to her family, explaining where she was going.

Retracing her stealthy steps down the hall, she found her shoes again by feeling with her toes and, leaning against the wall, put them on.

Pausing for only a moment to make certain all was still quiet and that the cats weren't nearby, she unlocked the front door and hurried into the entryway. She took the time to lock the dead bolt behind her before heading out the storm door and carefully cushioning its motion with her hand, preventing its usual bang against the jamb.

Cold enveloped Zoe with icy arms. She made her way to the wooden handrail, slick with a very thin coat of ice, and held on as her feet sought secure purchase on each step down to the driveway.

Car windows were fogged and icy. As the last one in, Zoe had parked in the turnaround, the farthest spot from the house. Rather than scraping the ice from the windows and making noise, she let the car engine clear the glass. Within a few minutes, she eased the old Chevy up the rutted drive.

Turning right when she reached the narrow paved road, she drove toward Beverage. Tree limbs and splinters lay across the asphalt or alongside it. Where earlier, the strong silhouette of an old oak had marked a hidden driveway, Zoe saw only a jagged streak of trunk surrounded by branches touching not sky but ground.

An uprooted maple blocked one lane of the two-lane highway, but there was no other car on the road as Zoe detoured into the oncoming lane to avoid it.

Once through Beverage, the interstate was clear, and Zoe dared to give the car enough gas to reach the speed limit. By the clock on her dashboard, it was close to 4:30 when she turned past the McKenna farm and eased down Ethan's private drive.

As she rounded the bend above Ethan's house, the place seemed mostly untouched by the storm, and she switched off the headlights. Not daring to creep closer with road debris crunching under her tires, Zoe reluctantly turned off the engine and left her car blocking the road. She wished she could come up with a way to turn the thing around, in the event she needed a quick escape, but that could not be accomplished without pulling down to the gravel parking area beside the house.

As she crept down the drive, she saw that the water level of the lake had risen, but it did not threaten Ethan's house.

The garage door was locked, just as it had been, but that told Zoe nothing. Sliding around the side of that outbuilding, she approached Ethan's house obliquely. The place was dark, the windows vacant.

On the front porch, Zoe took a deep breath. Ethan's key was on the ring with her car keys and her own house keys. For a moment, she panicked at finding her pocket empty, before realizing the bundle of keys was clutched tightly in her left hand.

She fumbled only briefly with the lock, then turned the knob and stepped inside. Flattening herself against the wall, Zoe peered into the darkness, waiting for her eyes to adjust. No sound other than her own hammering heart reached her ears.

The walk across the floor seemed to take forever, as she carefully checked for squeaky floorboards before shifting her weight to one leg or the other. The stairs were no better, and in some ways worse, for sometimes the entire stair creaked; avoiding it meant skipping that one and stepping on untested treads. Zoe held her breath as she neared the top.

Just as she reached the upstairs hallway and dared to gulp down enough air to get her the rest of the way to the bedroom, the hall light flashed on with all the brilliance a sixty-watt bulb can supply.

"Don't make a move!" a male voice boomed. "I'm armed."

Zoe's arms flew up of their own volition. Still blinded by the sudden cessation of night, she blinked furiously. Quicksand seemed to encase her legs because the floor was suddenly unsteady beneath her feet. She struggled to find her voice. "Don't shoot! I'm Ethan's cousin Zoe. You've been looking for me!"

"You sure you're okay?" Whitby Marshall asked.

Zoe nodded at the handsome man sitting across the kitchen table from her. The bathrobe Zoe had seen hanging on the door of the smaller bedroom was securely tied around his waist. The sweats he'd been wearing, emblazoned with the words "Bickle County Sheriff's Department," had been perfectly respectable, but he had hastily pulled the robe on.

With an unsteady hand, he poured a small amount of brandy into two juice glasses and set one in front of her. For the moment, much as Zoe thought it might calm her down just a notch, her hands shook too violently to even attempt reaching for the glass.

"I'm fine. Are you okay?" Her teeth still chattered involuntarily.

They looked at each other's faces, where terror was still fading, and laughed in a way that had little to do with humor and everything to do with adrenaline.

"I thought Ethan must have mentioned my name."

"Never."

A sudden smile took hold of Whitby's features, and he shook his head. "The fact that he keeps a promise almost got us in even deeper doo-doo, without him here to explain things. Are you sure you're okay? You're very pale."

"I'm fine." She attempted putting her hands on either side of the glass. They twitched uncontrollably.

"We're both in shock. I was even expecting you, just not in the middle of the night. Ethan said you were one of the best investigators the Justice Department ever had. I thought it was just his pride talking."

"It was," Zoe said with a tired smile. Her lips had trouble falling back over her teeth.

"How did you figure it out?"

"I'm not sure. I looked for your car—which I presume is in the garage?—at every motel and bed and breakfast in Bickle County. When that didn't pan out, I even called the Feller County sheriff for some assistance. After that, I guess I was just thinking about where a person could hide a silver Jaguar. Everyone's talking about the car. You couldn't just park it under a tree and hope no one would notice. The answer popped into my head while I slept. I'd seen that bathrobe on the door when I came here. It wasn't Ethan's. That—and the trash. You'd cleaned up. First, I thought someone was trying to hide something. But why go to all the trouble of throwing the perishables out? Anything that could be hidden by mixing it with garbage was something that could have been taken away. None of it made sense until I realized you had to be staying here." After a failed attempt to lift her brandy, Zoe said, "What did you mean about a promise Ethan made to you?"

"I asked him to keep quiet about us, not to tell anyone. I work for the FBI, mostly at the National Academy at Quantico, training law enforcement officers, which was how Ethan and I met. I've got some seniority under my belt, believe me, but I've been hesitant about coming out. Things between Ethan and me were going very well, and I knew he wanted you to meet me, but he was waiting for me to bring it up. I have to admit, I didn't trust him as much as he warranted, because I figured he would have told you about me and just asked you to keep it under your hat."

"Not Ethan," Zoe said, savoring that image of her cousin.

"No, not Ethan. You need some help with that brandy? A straw, maybe?"

She laughed. "If I lift this glass, it's going to spill down the front of me."

"Here." He grabbed a dish towel from under the sink and tucked it, bib-like, under Zoe's chin. Resuming his seat, he shakily lifted his own glass and gestured toward her with it. "Go to town."

Using both hands, she managed to get it to her lips.

"To Ethan's recovery," Whitby said, not even attempting to touch his glass to hers. Zoe noticed that his hand was only slightly steadier than her own.

"Yes. To Ethan's recovery." The glass clattered against her teeth, but Zoe managed to swallow a sip of the brandy. It burned nicely through her chest, jump-starting her own thermostat, she hoped. She took another sip before carefully returning the glass to the table.

"That old address of mine you have. Did that come from Ethan's book?"

"No. You're not in his address book. I guess he figured yours was one he knew. I did find your phone number jotted down on the inside cover of the book, but every time I called over there—and always from a phone booth, in case you have caller I.D.—you were out. A few times, I got your answering machine. Not knowing who might be at your house, I didn't dare leave a message."

Whitby paused to sip appreciatively at the brandy, "Anyway, I finally had a friend in the Justice Department look up your old record. That's where I got the address. I figured you'd find out about that."

"A year or two back, we all got street addresses, to make it easier for emergency personnel to find houses in the back of beyond, like mine. My new address is in the database at Justice, but I guess no one bothered to note it on paper.

"Why haven't you let the local police know who you are? The official investigation is mired down in proving that Rosalyn Fitzgerald's husband did the shooting. Based on no evidence whatsoever, they think Ethan and Rosalyn were having an affair."

"I've read the papers." He took another sip of the brandy. "I haven't stuck my nose into local doings because, officially, I'm on vacation. And because I wasn't sure who might be involved in the shooting. I'm still not sure. I'm going to call a friend and suggest the investigation be taken over by a more experienced agent."

"You've been nosing around the county, though. You must have found out some things."

"I found out you taped a high school basketball game. Nearly scared the heck out of me when the VCR powered itself up the other day. When it was finished, I checked out the tape. My guess is the game was important to you for reasons other than fanatic devotion to the local team."

The hand that reached for the glass in front of Zoe was much steadier. She even managed to nod after sipping and returning the glass safely to the table. "There's a young woman who lives across the creek from Rosalyn Fitzgerald's house. The star quarterback of the high school team says he saw her at the basketball game the afternoon of the shootings. I've watched reruns of that game a couple of times. I can't see him or her in the bleachers. And either one of them would stand out. She goes to the creek often. It's far from her house, there's a huge blue spruce that provides some shelter, and no one can see her while she smokes pot. I think she saw something across the creek that afternoon. She wouldn't have been able to see the actual shootings because of the way the driveway curves behind a rise, but she sure could have seen the shooter. She says there were two men, but only one had a gun."

Zoe shrugged. "The young woman lies. Regularly. I'm sure she knows the difference between lying and telling the truth, but I'm not sure she can stop herself from telling a story. It's habit now. But I do think she's a bona fide witness."

"Ren Bertram," Whitby supplied, since Zoe had not. "She buys marijuana, and maybe something else, from the custodian at the local high school. Two packages. One she pockets. The other she slips to a well-built, blond young man. Your quarterback, I presume. Maybe he pays her later, but I sure didn't see any money change hands in that transaction."

"Ah," Zoe said, drawing out the syllable. "That ever so nicely gives us a motive for Billy Johns, our blond young man, to want to lie for Ren. Even when she didn't ask him to. He doesn't want to lose his supplier."

"What do you think? Painkillers?"

"Yes, maybe. Or maybe some kind of steroids." Billy Johns' wide shoulders muscled into her thoughts.

"So what's next on your agenda? Another round of questioning with Ren?"

"Her mother called the police about my interrogating Ren. So did the mother's lawyer. I've officially been warned off."

"Well, I haven't. And I've got some legitimacy backing me up. How about you come along with me tomorrow—today—and we have a little talk with Ren Bertram?"

"I'd like that, but it'll blow your anonymity."

"I think it's time for that. I've been lucky up until now. I should have rented another car, but I just love that Jag. Nothing else drives like it."

"There's something else," Zoe said, for the first time feeling the brandy hit her brain and yawning widely. Crumpling the towel that she snatched from around her neck, she bunched it on the table. "There was a drug bust planned to go down on the same day that Ethan was shot. The task force was set up at an abandoned farm off the Pumpkin Cave exit of the interstate. The Feller County sheriff told me it never happened because of the shootings, but I wonder if there isn't some connection. I'll bet Pumpkin Cave doesn't see that much excitement in ten years, let alone in one afternoon. Tomorrow—this morning—the sheriff is supposed to fax me directions to the site where the sting was going to occur.

"The state narc, Andrew Prescott, told me he's been posing as a supplier. He was supposed to meet the local supplier at the sting. He and the other members of the task force have been very careful to keep mum on the name of the local dealer they've been cultivating, but I'll bet I can guess who it is, after hearing your story about Ren."

"The custodian at the Bickle County school. His name is Bob Farmer. He also works Saturdays and special events at the Feller County high school. He deals there, too."

"Isn't it interesting how Ren plays a part in both the drugs and the shootings? I think we're not getting the full story on either side."

"Okay. Ren will be in school today. At least, she should be. Why don't we go check out the place where the sting was to have taken place? Then we'll interview Ren. First, though, could you please make whatever arrangements are necessary to get me in to see Ethan?"

They drove in Zoe's car, the only way they could get to the hospital without police intervention. Witness to how Ethan didn't so much revive, but surge, upon seeing Whitby, Zoe discreetly stepped out into the hallway. With the private security guard occasionally stealing glances at her, Zoe stalked the corridors, her mind on more than her cousin's safety.

Afterward, Whitby was very quiet. Zoe left him to his thoughts as they drove up the interstate. She was enjoying the uncommon sight of sunlight reflecting brilliantly on every available surface, including the dirty hood of her car. Air whistled at the vents and open windows, caressing faces and arms with a warming breeze.

Evidence of the power of the storms of the previous few days was more than visible in the debris along the road and, in one spot, the buckling of the pavement, but the drive itself was quick and uneventful.

"This is our exit," Zoe said at last, breaking the quiet. "I'll need you to be navigator now."

Whitby nodded and referred to the fax he held in his hand. "At the stop sign at the end of the ramp, turn north. Go straight for a while."

As they approached the narrow bridge on the left, the place where Willa had lost her sense of direction when she had taken Zoe to see the scene of the shooting, Zoe slowed. She looked to Whitby. "Don't we turn left here?"

She'd been certain the abandoned farmhouse she and Willa had stumbled upon was the one the task force had picked for their sting. That put it very close to Rosalyn's house. Maybe someone had seen something. Maybe another drug dealer had been trailing the first, and somehow he had spotted Ethan and Rosalyn. Zoe's mind entertained all kinds of far-fetched possibilities, but they were all useless speculation if the old farmhouse wasn't the place they were looking for.

Whitby shook his head. "Not here. It's a right turn onto a bridge that we want to make. Up there, that looks like it."

"Are you sure that's what the directions say?"

"Want a look at them?"

Zoe shook her head. "I'm sorry. I don't doubt you. I just had a hypothesis I hate to lose . . ."

"You're going to pass it! Turn right!"

Zoe did as he asked, but her stomach fell. The air turned from pleasantly cool to dank and chill. She stopped the car. "Then we stay on this lane, right? Until we go left and the road curves in front of the farmhouse?"

"Yeah, that's pretty much it, but these directions mention that the porch is sagging, and a few of the windows are missing. Have you been here before?"

"It's Rosalyn Fitzgerald's house we're going to," Zoe said. "But not with the missing windows and the sagging porch. That one's across the street, at the left-turn bridge."

"What?"

Zoe took a deep breath and let it out. Softly, she repeated, "We're being directed to Rosalyn Fitzgerald's house. I'll show you."

Taking her foot off the brake, she followed the narrow lane past the public fishing area and the blue spruce across the creek. New windows gleamed in the sun as Zoe pulled around the house and up the driveway. As she put the car in park, she turned to Whitby, puzzlement spreading across her face.

Whitby reached for the door handle. "This is the scene of the shooting?"

Zoe nodded. "We're parked just about where Ethan was. The shooter stood up there, hidden behind that line of hemlocks."

"What's it mean? There's no way this place could be mistaken for an abandoned farmhouse. Anyone coming in could see from the condition of the front lawn that this place is occupied."

"Clear the car, Whitby!" Zoe cried, reaching for her door. "There's someone behind those trees!"

They bailed out together, and when they met at the back of the car, Whitby's semiautomatic was in his hand. He demanded hoarsely, "Where?"

Keeping low, Zoe pointed. It could have been exactly where Ethan's assailant had stood.

"I'm a federal agent!" Whitby shouted, pointing the weapon with both hands. "Raise your hands and come on out."

After a seemingly interminable pause, Ren Bertram stepped through the line of trees, a fishing rod in her hand. The red streak in her hair standing out even more than usual due to her unnatural pallor, she stood before them, her lips trembling.

"Drop the fishing rod," Whitby commanded.

Ren looked at the thing as if unaware she held it in her hand. With a gasp, she flung it down. Then her wide eyes returned to Whitby.

He lowered the gun and reholstered it after several tries. Holding out his shaking hands, he glanced ruefully at Zoe and said, "I've never pulled my weapon so often in my entire career!"

Ren had simply collapsed to a sitting position on the wet ground.

Zoe hurried up the hill and, with an arm around Ren's shoulders, helped her back to her feet. The young woman roused herself, surprised to see Zoe. "I thought that guy was going to kill me!"

"And we thought you were going to kill us! Can you make it to the driveway? I've got a blanket in the trunk of my car."

"I don't need any blanket. I heard the car drive up, and I was just interested in seeing who it was. I thought maybe it was the murderers coming back. Or maybe my cousin."

Zoe leaned Ren against the trunk of her car. "This is Whitby

Marshall. He's a federal agent, Ren. Agent Marshall, this is Ren Bertram."

"Charmed, I'm sure," Whitby said sarcastically. "What are you doing here, Ms. Bertram?"

"I was fishing," Ren said, gesturing toward her pole as if the answer had to be obvious.

"All you'd get in that creek today is flood debris," Zoe pointed out. "And you weren't on the bank when we drove by. Besides, I believe you'd be on the opposite side if fishing was your objective."

"You're cutting school, too," Whitby pointed out. "That's a serious offense on top of the trespass."

"What were you doing, Ren?" Zoe pressed.

"I told you, I was fishing! I *was* on the bank, but when I heard the car tires on the road, I ran and hid. I was afraid the guys I saw before were coming back to get me!"

"Let's have a look, why don't we?" Zoe said, climbing up the small, slippery hill of the front lawn.

She headed straight for the front porch, where she expected to see at least a front window jimmied open. If Ren couldn't climb in to get what she wanted, Zoe figured she might be using the fishing pole to try to snag something inside. But the windows were all closed. The door, too, was secure.

Ren and Whitby had come to stand by the porch as Zoe checked the house. She walked all the way around the place, but found nothing that looked as if it had been forced open.

"What were you doing, Ren?" she asked again, but this time rhetorically, as she clambered off the porch and took off across the wide front lawn.

"I was fishing in the creek!" Ren cried. "Why won't you believe me? I like to fish!"

Zoe laughed, but there was no joy in it. "So do I, Ren. For liars. And I think I've hooked me a big one."

She swiveled her gaze, looking for something that would snag her attention.

"Over there," Whitby pointed. The lawn was dotted with out-buildings, but Whitby had singled out what looked like a low shed across from the parking area.

As the three approached, Zoe could see that it wasn't a shed but a very short structure constructed of two-by-fours, maybe two feet tall and about fifteen or more feet in diameter. The top was closed off with more two-by-fours, except for one board in the middle that had warped. It stuck up at an odd angle and was obviously the anomaly that had caught Whitby's eye.

The thing looked like a too-low primitive banquet table or a too-high dance floor.

With a quizzical glance toward Ren, Zoe tested the top by lean-ing on it with her hands. Then she gingerly climbed up on it.

"Don't go that way!" Ren cried as tears began rolling down her cheeks. "There are loose boards right in front of you! You'll fall in!"

Already on her knees, Zoe stopped. She took her Swiss Army knife from her pocket, opened the awl, and tried to pry up the board immediately before her. It didn't budge, but the one beside it did.

"What is it?" Whitby asked.

Carefully, Zoe lifted the loose board and set it beside her. The next board also came off, and then the warped one.

"It's an old well," Ren offered.

"I don't think so," Zoe said, shaking her head. "It's too big for a well. I think it's an air shaft to an old mine."

She looked around her. "Can you grab a good-sized stone some-where?"

Whitby obliged. Leaning carefully over the opening she had made near the center of the boards, Zoe dropped the stone. It was several seconds before they all heard the plop of it hitting water far below.

"Hah! I told you it was a well!" Ren declared.

"No, it's an air shaft, Ren. It's just filled with water."

"But mines don't have water in them! How would miners get at the coal?"

"Most coal mines do have water in them, Ren, because they're so deep. The water gets pumped out when the mine is working, but once it's closed down and the openings are sealed, the water comes back."

"How do you know that?" Ren asked, not altogether convinced.

"Because I've seen my share of these things. My dad worked as a miner." Still kneeling, Zoe turned from the hole to face Ren. "What is it you were fishing for in here?"

"Why would I be fishing in a mine shaft?"

Zoe nodded, as if she had expected no other answer. Carefully crawling to the edge of the platform, she swung her legs to the ground. "Agent Marshall, I don't think you have any choice but to take this young woman into custody. Maybe once she's under guard, she'll think twice about lying and obstructing justice."

Zoe lowered her head, as if in sadness. "I'm sorry, Ren. I tried to help you."

Ren stomped one foot, but tears made dirty rivulets down her cheeks. "You can't arrest me! My mother says you can't even come near me!"

"I'm not doing anything, Ren. That's the responsibility of this gentleman. He'll make sure your mother is notified. She can bring her lawyer along when she comes to visit you."

"Let's go, Ms. Bertram," Whitby Marshall said, reaching for Ren's arm. "You can come with me while I put in a call for a squad car."

Ren wrenched her arm from his grasp. Tears coursed harder down her face as she cried, "Please don't arrest me! My mother said she'd send me away if it happened again."

She sobbed as if her heart would break, and Zoe had to restrain the impulse to comfort her.

"It was the gun!" Ren cried, sinking to the ground. "He threw the gun in there! They ran down the lawn, the two of them, and they were yelling at each other, but I couldn't hear what they said! They ran to the car, and then the one who lost his hat looked over at the board that was sticking up. He said something to the other guy, and then he came over here and dropped the gun in. He waited until he heard it hit the water, just the way you did with that rock. Then he threw in something else—I don't know what. It looked like a handful of pebbles that he got out of his pocket. And then he replaced the board and ran back to the car, where—"

Ren paused for only a heartbeat before picking up the narrative again. "Where the other guy was already in the car. They turned the car around and just peeled out. Gravel went flying everywhere!"

She sniffled, wiping at her nose with the back of her hand. "That's all I know."

"Who drove the car, Ren?" Zoe prodded gently.

"The guy who had the gun."

"What did the car look like, Ms. Bertram?" Whitby asked.

"It was a blue Neon. I saw the round headlights; that's how I know. The driver's door was a different shade of blue than the rest of the car."

"Are you certain, Ren?" Zoe asked gently. "It wasn't a white pickup truck?"

"The white truck is my stupid cousin's. He wasn't there. It was a blue Neon."

"Now tell us about the two men," Zoe prodded. "Did you know both of them?"

Miserably, Ren shook her head. "If I tell you, he'll kill me. And if I don't tell you, I go to jail."

"He'll be the one in jail, Ren. You'll be protected." Zoe glanced at Whitby Marshall, who nodded. "Who was he, Ren?"

"Farmer Bob," Ren whispered to her chest.

"Who?"

"I call him Farmer Bob," Ren said in the threadiest of voices. Her fingers clutched at the wet grass. "His name is Bob Farmer. He's a janitor at school."

"How do you know him, Ren?"

Whitby Marshall handed the young woman a red handkerchief that Zoe knew had come from Ethan's drawer. Ren blew her nose, then clutched the square of material in her fist.

"He's not nice. He threatens me all the time. He's scary."

"I know, Ren, but we need your help to get him locked up where he can't scare you anymore. How do you know him?"

Ren shook her head, her expression pleading with Zoe to stop the torture. "I just know him from school, okay?"

"I'm sorry, Ren. That's not good enough."

"Oh, what am I going to do?"

"We'll help you, Ren. How do you know him?"

Tears burbled afresh from her eyes, and Ren succumbed to sobbing. This time, it was Whitby who made a move toward comforting her, but Zoe, feeling her stomach twist, shook her head, warning him off.

Once she had herself under control again, Ren said, "Please, just let me go. I promise I'll never get in trouble again."

"How do you know him, Ren?" Zoe repeated.

"I buy marijuana from him." She dropped her chin to her chest.

"What else?"

"What else?"

"Yes, what else do you buy from him?"

"GHB. It's for building muscles."

"What?" Zoe asked, taken aback. She'd expected to hear a name she recognized.

"One of the date-rape drugs," Whitby Marshall supplied.

"He'd never use it for that," Ren said steadfastly.

Zoe asked, "You're certain it was Bob Farmer you saw running down this lawn on the day Deputy Fitzgerald and Sheriff McKenna were shot?"

"Yes, I'm certain! I was right over there, under the spruce tree! I was kind of dreaming, not paying much attention. Then I heard shooting, just a couple of pops. I thought someone was out hunting, and I didn't think any more about it. After that, I saw Sheriff McKenna drive by. I figured Rosalyn was with him. Someone or other was always bringing her home because there was something wrong with her car. Then I heard more shots, and I saw those two men come barreling down the lawn, just like I said."

"You heard shots before the sheriff drove up?"

"Yes." Ren sniffled.

"Did you recognize the other man, Ren?"

"No! I told you, no!"

"Could you recognize him if you saw him again?"

"I don't know. He had long hair and a beard."

"What color was his hair?"

"I don't know. It was kind of lightish, but not blond."

When no one said anything for a moment, Ren added, "Please don't take me to jail."

Zoe looked to Whitby, who frowned and shook his head.

He said, "It'll never hold up in court. She was stoned."

Ren shot to her feet, tugging her sweatshirt down at the waist. "Maybe I'd smoked a little, but I wasn't stoned. And I wasn't stoned when Bob Farmer threatened me with that date-rape drug."

Whitby pulled at his ear, thinking. At last he said, "We'll take you home, Ms. Bertram. Then we'll wait until another agent arrives."

"No, please don't take me home! There's no one there now, and I hate that house! It's so big, anyone could get in! Please!"

"How about your cousin's house?"

"No!" Ren said defiantly and—Zoe observed—fearfully.

"We can't take her to Russell Creek," Whitby said, referring to the sheriff's department. "At least not until we get one or two more things straight."

"My house," Zoe said with a sigh. "It's crawling with siblings and assorted hangers-on. You won't be lonely there, Ren. And we can still call for backup from your department, Agent Marshall."

"I've got an agent in Feller County now. It shouldn't take her long to get to your place."

"What put you on to Ren in the first place?" Zoe asked, taking her eyes from the road for only a moment to watch Whitby's reaction.

They had left Ren with Zoe's brother David and sister Miriam. After some awkwardness, Ren had agreed to play cards. It turned out she'd learned pinochle, the Kergulins' favorite game, during detention at school. A spirited hand was in progress as Zoe and Whitby slipped away.

"One of the state police detectives told me he kept getting the odor of marijuana at the crime scene, but there was absolutely no evidence of leaves or seeds or ashes. I checked out a map, found out who lived across the way, and then found out the ages of the family members. Ren was my first choice."

Zoe nodded admiringly. "Well done. Did you turn up anything on her cousin, Ellis Anton?"

"Yeah. His family's rich, probably the richest one in Bickle County. That's it."

"No marijuana connection?"

"Nothing that ties him to Bob Farmer. At least nothing I saw."

"Well, Ren doesn't like him. I didn't care for him much myself."

"It would be kind of hard to get a warrant based on that." He twisted in his seat, flexing his shoulders as if the muscles were too tight. "You think the shooter is Bob Farmer's supplier?"

"Things sure point to him. He was supposed to be at that meeting."

"But what would he be doing at Rosalyn's house?"

"That's the million-dollar question, isn't it?"

Whitby's credentials immediately got them in to see Shep Tuttle, who broke up a staff meeting that had just begun.

He greeted them in an effusive, if somewhat puzzled, manner. "You know, I just got a message for you from someone named Ren that you're supposed to call your house, Miss Zoe. I wondered why anyone would call here looking for you, but she said you were on your way. I hope it's not bad news."

Zoe quickly dialed her own number. "David, it's Zoe . . . What?. . . Oh, geez. Okay, bye."

Exasperatedly, she shook her head. "I only have crunchy peanut butter. She only eats smooth. I apologize for the interruption, Sheriff."

"No problem. What can I do for you?"

Zoe spread out the somewhat worn fax in front of the sheriff. "You gave us directions to Rosalyn Fitzgerald's house."

"What?" Shep Tuttle asked, scratching his head.

"The directions you had faxed to me this morning, the ones that were supposed to show us where your meeting place was, led us right to Rosalyn Fitzgerald's place."

"The dead deputy?"

"That's the one."

"Well, hell, Miss Zoe, we all knew where the meeting was supposed to be. I really only had the directions typed up so we'd have something in the file. I get lefts and rights mixed up sometimes, but it doesn't have any bearing on the sting or on the shooting."

"Sheriff," Whitby Marshall said, settling back in his chair and tugging gently at Zoe's sweater to get her seated, too. He crossed ankle over knee and straightened the crease on his trousers. "Why don't you tell us who was in your party, waiting at the abandoned house?"

"Well, it was me, of course, and Chickie Ondean's son, Kendall—he's the liaison with the Bickle County folks—and then there was my deputy, Todd Dickerson. Andrew Prescott's boss—Rick something-or-other, Rodriguez or Sanchez, something like that—was in the van with the equipment."

Whitby laid a hand on the arm of Zoe's chair, as if to restrain her. "And who was supposed to be coming to this meeting place?"

"Well, sir, it was Andrew Prescott, who's been busting his butt on this case. He's a state narc, forced to work in what I know must be a backwater for him, but he's doing a fine job, just a fine job. He's been passing himself off as a small-time drug supplier. And then there's a dealer we know about, but he's cornered a totally different market, crossing between Bickle and Feller Counties."

"Bob Farmer is supplying drugs to kids."

A look of surprise flooded Shep Tuttle's face. "Well, yes, he is. We were aiming to get him on some pretty hefty charges, just as soon as the sting went down."

"Who else?" Whitby prompted.

"The guy who supplies Bob Farmer. We only know him as Skid. He's the one we were really looking to take down."

"Were Farmer, Prescott, and Skid arriving together?"

"No. As I recall, Farmer called Andrew early that day. He said he couldn't get his car started, and he couldn't get hold of Skid. So he asked Andrew to come by and pick him up. When Andrew got there, Skid had already called back and said he'd swing by to pick up Farmer. So Farmer told Andrew to go on out to the meeting place, and he and Skid would be along directly."

"Sounds like they might have been setting your boy up," Whitby observed.

"It's possible, although we try to do what we can to avoid those kinds of situations. Actually, Andrew says he thought they passed him on the interstate. He's not sure, but he thinks it was them. Then, a little ways outside of Pumpkin Cave, he pulled up with a flat. He couldn't get the damn lug nuts off; you know how tight they put them on at the stations. They use that compressor thing. Anyway, by the time he finally managed to stand on the jack and get the flat off and the spare on, it was too late. He didn't have a radio with him on purpose, in case Farmer checked. And Farmer had specified no cell phones so he couldn't contact us until he drove in."

"And Farmer and Skid?"

"That was the strange thing. They never showed. Maybe they did suspect a setup, but while we were all jawing over what we should do next, our dispatch picked up the call about Sheriff McKenna. We just called everything off.

"All that planning, all that advance work, and it just petered out in front of us. O' course, we'll be setting it up again soon. That explains why Mr. Farmer's still in business. We'll be getting him, though, you bet."

"What kind of car was Andrew Prescott driving?"

Tuttle shrugged. He moved his jaw as if chewing cud. "I don't know for sure. It was a confiscated vehicle, I know that. Mr. Prescott told me it had been taken from drug dealers, and he was using it to put good karma back into it." Sheriff Tuttle smiled.

"He's a card, that one."

"Who picked the meeting place?"

"I've been thinking on that since Miss Zoe here asked that same question. Andrew and Farmer together, I think, with maybe some input from Skid and members of our team. I know that's rather broad, but I'm just not sure."

Whitby slowly nodded. Zoe could see that his teeth were working at the inside of his cheek. He returned his foot to the floor and leaned forward. "Do you know what kind of car this Skid character was driving?"

"No, I don't think so. I'm not sure Andrew knows. I don't believe he put it in his report."

"You have any idea what Skid looks like?"

"None at all, sir. Andrew, he says he thought he recognized Farmer in the passenger seat of the car that passed him, but he didn't get a good look at Skid. All he could say was that it looked like the fellow was wearing one of those knitted hats."

"Did Skid or Farmer get a copy of your directions to the meeting place?"

The sheriff leaned back in his chair as if pushed. "Why would they need to have that? They helped pick the meeting place!"

"You're certain about everything you've told us, Sheriff?"

"Well, I'm pretty sure. Let me buzz my secretary, and she'll find Mr. Prescott's report for you."

"So?" Whitby asked, waiting for Zoe to slide behind the wheel.

"So, if it's so easily solved, why did it take us coming along to crack the case? And why is Kirk Fitzgerald sitting in jail?"

After a brief pause, both Whitby and Zoe spoke in unison. "And—"

"You go," Whitby said, smiling.

"Okay. If I sold drugs for a living, and I went with my distributor—for whatever reason—to a farmhouse that obviously was not abandoned, and I saw a white car clearly labeled 'Sheriff,' complete with red and blue lights on the roof, coming down the driveway, I think I'd say, 'Hey, this is a setup.' And maybe I would shoot whoever was in that car. But first I'd kill the person or persons I thought had set me up: the distributor, Farmer."

"Exactly. And, if Ren's telling the truth, Bob Farmer wasn't the one wearing the cap. Let's go make a few calls. I want to find out who drives a blue Plymouth Neon."

"Okay, thanks," Whitby said and hung up the phone. He stepped out of the booth to Zoe.

"If we'd taken my car," he said, "we'd have our own phone."

Zoe nodded. "I don't usually need one. So, tell me."

"The confiscated car is a blue Plymouth Neon with a distinctive driver's side door of a deeper shade of blue."

"Andrew was the one in the cap," Zoe said, her mouth going dry.

"I think so. I can't figure a motive for him to be gunning for Ethan, though. Can you?"

Zoe began to shake her head but stopped in midmotion. "Oh, no!" Feeling her insides grow cold, she continued, "I don't know if Sheriff Tuttle really likes Andrew as much as he seems to. I have a hard time reading the guy. I never know when he's playing to the audience and when he's not. But Andrew Prescott doesn't like Tuttle at all. The first day I met him, in the hospital just after Ethan was shot, he came into the I.C.U. and sat down next to me—newly shorn and shaved. Under the guise of telling me how much he admired Ethan, he compared the sheriffs of Feller and Bickle Counties. The sheriff of Feller County did not fare well. I can't remember the entire list, but one thing that stood out that terrible day was that he said Sheriff Tuttle was dyslexic. I remember thinking, so what? Why would anyone be upset about dyslexia? The guy can't help having it, can he?

"But it would be important to Andrew if Tuttle's dyslexia resulted in garbled directions to this meeting place that Andrew had worked on setting up for months—months without showering much, shaving less, and living a not very nice life, I'm sure. Whitby, what do you think Prescott and Farmer were doing out at Rosalyn Fitzgerald's house?"

"Following Shep Tuttle's written instructions. The question is—why?"

They studied each other for a few moments. Zoe leaned against her car. "Maybe he was hoping to show Shep Tuttle up as a bungler."

"That might work, except that Prescott did know where the sting was supposed to take place." Whitby chewed on his lower lip.

"Let's not forget the bigger question. Where was Skid? Isn't Skid the person this whole operation was arranged around? If Skid was given a copy of Shep Tuttle's directions, why didn't he show up at the Fitzgerald place? Ren only saw Farmer and Prescott."

"Maybe he got wind of the bust," Whitby postulated.

"If he did, why not simply cancel the planned meeting? Why let Farmer, one of the guys who sells drugs for him, take a fall?"

"Skid could have thought Farmer was in on the sting."

"Or," Zoe said, her face lighting up as she raised a finger, "maybe someone warned Skid off."

"Someone inside, you're saying. A cop."

"Think about it, Whitby. There's one narc dead. That could point to a police officer who's feeding information to the bad guys. And Skid not showing up could be further support for that hypothesis."

"Then when did Skid get warned off? And why didn't he show up at Fitzgerald's house?"

"Maybe the contact in the police department didn't know about the sting until it went down. Then the officer would have had to scramble in order to get word to Skid."

"But there were supposed to be no cell phones," Whitby pointed out. "How would Skid find out?"

"How about a marked patrol car? If I wanted to alert a crony that trouble lurked at a meeting place, I would simply park my cruiser somewhere near a designated site. I wouldn't have to say a word. The bad guy would see me and just keep on driving. Might even throw me a wave, like any other friendly citizen."

"Then we need to find out if anyone saw someone waiting at the right place."

Whitby saw revelation land on Zoe's features.

"I've got it, Whitby! If Skid went to Fitzgerald's place, maybe Andrew would know that there was no one feeding information to him, because he would've simply been following the directions provided. Perhaps that's what Andrew was hoping for. If, however, Skid showed up where the sting was supposed to occur, then it's a good bet someone else was giving him instructions."

"Okay. That would explain Prescott's presence at the Fitzgerald place. But it sure doesn't explain the shooting."

"No, it doesn't," Zoe agreed, disappointed to have her thread run out so quickly. Suddenly, she grabbed Whitby's arm and fastened a bleak gaze on him. "Oh, no, Whitby. What do you think was the first thing Tuttle did after we left his office?"

"Probably spilled everything we told him to whoever the inside contact is."

"Maybe, but I'm betting he called Andrew Prescott. You know Tuttle likes to shmooze. He'll tell him we were asking about the car. Prescott will know we're not buying the flat tire story. Tuttle will tell him we were interested in the directions that led to Rosalyn Fitzgerald's house. Then he'll tell him about some girl with a bird's name who called and told Miss Zoe to get some peanut butter without chunks.

"Whitby, if Andrew knows we know about the directions, and he knows we're giving Ren some credence, he might be desperate enough to go after her. He knows where I live. Thanks to Tuttle, he probably now knows Ren is there. My family's there, too."

Zoe dashed to the driver's door, where she threw herself behind the wheel. "Hurry up, Whitby! We've got to get out there!"

He dived into the car, barely managing to close the door as the car shot out into traffic.

"Wait, Zoe! You've got to stop and let me call for backup!"

"Who's going to get there in time?" Zoe considered calling Kip Chaney and asking her to get down the hill and tell everyone to evacuate up to Kip's, but that would put her friend in the middle of a potentially deadly situation.

"Zoe, I outrank Agent Gordon. She'll do what I ask. Plus, someone has to let Ren's mother know what's going on. We can't risk having her show up where she shouldn't be. And I've got to let the agent we put out at your house know not to let Andrew Prescott in, if he arrives before we do. Zoe, stop the car!"

The panic didn't ease, but Zoe let up on the gas. "Okay, okay. You're right. I'll pull over at the next phone booth."

"Zoe, are you okay?" David grabbed her by the shoulders.

She nodded, hollow-eyed. "What did the police say when they called?"

"They're on their way, but there have been a couple of mud slides. Their forces are diminished, dealing with other emergencies, and they're running a little behind."

"There's a mud slide on my driveway, too. It's too dangerous to try to get everyone out that way. I'm going to call Kip. She lives up on the George place. You remember the farm behind mine, up the hillside? We went berry picking there last summer."

His face lit up. "Sure, sure I remember. We just follow that little creek, right?"

"David, could you lead everyone up there? Kip will meet you, I'm sure. We've got to get everyone out of the house. There's a killer out there, and he could be shooting at anyone."

"You want us to take the cats?"

She threw her arms around him. "No. They'll hide if a stranger gets in. Just, please, make sure they don't get out when you all go. Let me call Kip. Meanwhile, you gather everyone together."

Zoe started down the hall for her office.

"Hey!" David called, stopping her. "What are you going to do?"

"We're taking Ren out by the driveway. She's got to be made safe. The federal agent who's been here and Whitby will be going, too. We'll take two cars. If one doesn't make it, the other will."

"Okay. Just let those feds handle the guy with the gun."

"Sounds fine to me."

"Tell your friend we're on our way."

There was a terrible moment when the thought flashed through Zoe's mind that Kip wasn't home, but she picked up the phone on the fourth ring.

"I was showering," Kip said breathlessly, explaining why it had taken her longer than usual to answer. "I was out shoveling mud earlier. You okay?"

Quickly, Zoe explained the dilemma.

"Send 'em on up," Kip heartily agreed. "I'm not sure where we'll all fit, but we'll find room. Want me to start off and meet them on the way?"

"Thanks, Kip. They're following the creek up. The sooner they're out of here, the better."

"Go on, Zoe. You get out of there, too. There's no way the guy is going to know about my house. Say, why don't you bring the girl up here, too? Why put yourself in danger?"

"We can't take the chance of leading the killer straight to your place, Kip. It's enough you're saving my family."

"It's Stephanie. Stephanie Felder. The name I was born with, the one I can't use anymore. I've been wanting to tell you for what seems the longest time. You're the best friend I've ever had, Zoe. Now, see that you stay alive to keep my secret."

When they told Ren to get in the car with Whitby, she responded emphatically. "No, I'm riding with Zoe. And I'm sitting in front. I can get down on the floor if I have to. If I ride in the back, I'll get carsick."

"You didn't get carsick before," Whitby pointed out.

"I hadn't just eaten then," Ren bristled defiantly.

"Okay," Whitby gave in. "You ride with Zoe. In the front. Agent Mann and I will take the first car. If we meet anyone on the way out, you let us handle him. Zoe, you just start reversing down the drive. Can you navigate that way? Then make your way to your friend's house."

She nodded, already climbing behind the wheel. "Put on the seat belt, Ren."

"They make me uncomfortable."

"And your point? Put on the seat belt."

"Looks like rain again," Ren announced, squinting out the windshield as she fastened the seat belt.

The white sedan backed into the turnaround behind Zoe, then gingerly pulled out around her. Quickly, Zoe swung in behind.

The going was slow. Near impassable in the best of times, the drive had turned into an obstacle course and, in some spots, a swamp. Despite her familiarity with every nuance of the ungraded path, despite her affection for the ruggedness that kept out casual visitors, Zoe found her hands gripping the wheel as if she expected it to try to get away from her at the first opportunity.

She swallowed, pushing down her fear, and said, "Ren, what kind of hold does Billy Johns have over you, to make you get him the GHB?"

Taken aback, Ren replied, "Hold? No hold. He's the cutest guy in school, and he likes me, Zoe. No one else even knows my name."

"Maybe it's time they did, Ren. Everyone needs a friend. Two or three are even better."

"Yeah, right. Well, I'm a freak, and no one wants a freak for a friend." Ren set her lips together. "Not that I want them, either."

"Ren, a true friend knows you by your heart."

"Ha-ha."

"You need a friend, Ren. Everyone does."

"You sound exactly like my cousin, Ellis. He wanted to be my friend, too. I'm not an idiot, you know."

The car ahead pivoted on a shelf of rock that had been on the hillside above the driveway only the day before. Like a sunning crocodile, it had crept off the shoulder of the road and come to rest on a flat piece of ground.

The undercarriage of Zoe's old Chevy hit slightly as she drove up the rock. Like the car in front, hers slid as it reached a slick puddle, bouncing back afterward to the hard clay where the tires made contact with the road once more.

"What did your cousin do under the pretext of friendship, Ren?"

"He didn't *do* anything. I don't know why I even brought up his name. I hate him."

"I know. I met him, and I didn't care too much for him, either."

Ren pressed her lips together with as much force as she had in her face. She glared at the car in front of them. Like a geyser, her anger burst out of her. Turning to Zoe, she spat, "Yeah, like he ever made you undress so he could take pictures of you!"

"Is that what he did to you, Ren? How old were you?"

The anger turned to tears. Ren hadn't expected anyone to believe her. Her mother never had, even on the day it happened. Ren had been sent to her room for telling such a story.

"I was around four or five," Ren sniffled. "I didn't want to do it. But he was bigger! He made me! And he kept taking pictures, even when I cried. Then he slapped me, and he told me to put my fingers where I didn't want to. But he made me! I didn't want to!

I didn't want to!"

Zoe's right hand had come to rest on Ren's shoulder, but Ren angrily shrugged it off. She sniffled again. "It was a long time ago. I should be over it by now."

"I'll bet it seems like yesterday whenever you think about him."

"Yeah, it does, but then I tell myself, you know, that he didn't rape me or anything. Except for slapping me, he didn't touch me at all."

"Oh, Ren, what he did to you was horrible!" Zoe turned the wheel sharply, and the car bounced into the edge of a pothole. "Did Billy Johns ever try anything like that with you?"

"Billy? No! I love him! He's never even touched me." Silent tears rolled down her cheeks.

"Well, we'll find a way to get your cousin. The police will be able to get a search warrant. They'll find what they need." Zoe was thinking that Ellis Anton had told Willa exactly the truth when he'd confessed that women had no appeal for him. No, he liked little girls instead. Zoe gritted her teeth at the thought. "With luck, he'll be put away for a long time, Ren. He won't be able to do to other little girls what he did to you."

"It wasn't just me? He told me it was just me. He told me I was bad."

"I'm sure it wasn't just you. And Ren, you weren't bad then, and you're not bad now."

"You believe me? Don't you know I'm the biggest liar ever to hit West Virginia?"

"I believe you, Ren. Maybe it's time to start thinking of yourself as the best storyteller ever to hit West Virginia."

The car in front pulled too far to the right, avoiding the worst of the mud slide, and the two outside wheels spun in the air for several seconds before gravity pulled them down again. Just when Zoe let out her breath, the sedan began to slide sideways before stopping against a tree.

Zoe threw her car into park, unbuckled the seat belt, and reached for the door. "Don't move, Ren. Stay right where you are."

As soon as she opened the door, Zoe heard similar instructions from Whitby. "We've got it under control here, Zoe. I just need to put a couple of rocks under the back tires. Stay in the car."

He glanced up the empty lane. "If anyone comes down, you stick it into reverse, just like we planned."

Zoe nodded and folded herself back into the car. She turned to face Ren.

In response, Ren unbuckled her own seat belt and stared at Zoe, silently daring her to say anything.

"We're about halfway up to the paved road," Zoe informed her. "It shouldn't take them long. They don't seem to be in too much of a jam."

Ren nodded. Using her palms, she wiped the dampness from her cheeks. "What's going to happen to me?" she asked in a very small voice.

"We'll see that you get to safety. Your mother will meet us when we get there. Bob Farmer will be arrested, and so will the man you saw with the gun. They won't have a chance to hurt you."

"How old do you have to be before you can buy a gun?"

Zoe shook her head. "With luck, Ren, you never reach that age, no matter how old you may be."

"What's that supposed to mean?"

Before she could answer, Zoe heard the sound of an engine. For a moment, it was impossible to tell if a car was getting closer or speeding away. Zoe saw Whitby straighten from a rock he'd been wrestling with. Like her, he listened, immobile.

Then he reached for his weapon, yelling at Agent Mann. "Get out of here!" he called to Zoe, waving both arms to emphasize the statement.

194

Zoe straightened behind the wheel even as she slammed the car into reverse. Sticking her arm across the back of Ren's seat, Zoe calmly instructed, "Hold on."

As she eased down on the gas, the tires spun. Despite the desperation that hammered at her, she calmly commented, "It's okay. Just a little mud."

She put the car into drive, turned the wheels just a bit, and gently touched the gas pedal. Once more, tires whined, but the car went nowhere.

"Okay," Zoe said, with a surreal calm she certainly did not feel, "this time should do it."

As she put the car into reverse once more, a blue Plymouth Neon roared down the drive toward them. It was a wonder Andrew Prescott had made it as far as he had, given the speed at which he was traveling. One round headlight and the fender on the same side had been smashed. Part of a tree branch protruded from just above the front bumper.

Zoe saw Whitby move as if in slow motion. Using the door as a shield, he pointed his gun. Whether he fired or not, she did not know. The roar of the Plymouth's engine absorbed all other sound.

The blue car smashed into the sedan, shoving it out of the way, and then the Neon was airborne, heading for the Chevy.

Without conscious thought, Zoe threw herself in front of Ren, clutching the young woman to her. She tensed, half-expecting the Plymouth to come flying through her own windshield.

What happened instead was the smash of the other car coming down engine first and bone-jarringly hard on the edge of the mud slide before gently rolling into Zoe's front bumper.

His suit, his shoes, his face, and his hair covered with mud, Whitby ran, limping, up to the passenger door of Zoe's car. He wrenched it open.

"Are you two okay?"

Zoe lifted herself from Ren's body enough to see the young woman nod tentatively. Then, realizing her own position in the car, she looked in amazement at Whitby.

She was practically sitting in Ren's lap, her left hand on Ren's cheek, trying to protect the young woman's head, her face close enough to Ren's to kiss, had she been so inclined.

Outside the car, Zoe heard Agent Mann calling for an ambulance for the unconscious Andrew Prescott. Relief engulfed her like a hot bath after a hard day. She studied her position again before grinning widely at Whitby.

He began to chortle.

"Hey, how about letting me breathe?" Ren said, pushing against Zoe. She looked from Zoe to Whitby and back to Zoe. "What?" she demanded testily. "What's so funny?"

Epilogue

"Prescott didn't have a flat tire."

Up until Ethan said the words, Zoe was not entirely sure he was following their explanation, although it was their second time through. His voice was hoarse, still rusty from disuse, but he sat up in bed with little help. If his face was drawn and somewhat gaunt, his eyes reflected none of that, flashing between Whitby and Zoe with a lively bounce. From her perch on the windowsill of Ethan's hospital room, Zoe beamed.

"No, he didn't," Whitby agreed. "The man was a genius at working his way into narcotics operations and busting them wide open in record time. Up until he met Sheriff Tuttle, anyway."

Zoe picked up the story. "We know from Andrew's superiors that he suspected Feller County police involvement in narcotics trafficking in that area. A narc was killed over there last year. Still unsolved. Andrew had to be on edge about that, probably thinking that the same thing could so easily happen to him. He proposed Shep Tuttle's name as a possible suspect and was laughed out of the office. It turns out Tuttle and two of the state narcs are buddies from way back, and the last thing they could envision was good old Shep being a bad guy."

Ethan blinked tiredly, but a contented smile relaxed the harsh lines painted on his face. His eyes came to rest on Whitby.

"We can finish next time," Zoe suggested.

Ethan shook his head. "Go on. Please."

"Okay," Whitby obliged. "Prescott voiced his fears often enough that his boss agreed to be part of the team when the sting went down. But Prescott wasn't satisfied. He complained it wasn't enough. He still thought his life was in danger. Apparently, he felt abandoned by his own department, fearful of the drug guys, and unable to trust Feller County police. Bob Farmer ratcheted up his fear by telling him the drug network had a guy on the inside. High up."

Zoe interjected, "It was the sharp eye of Kendall Ondean that noticed the Feller County police cruiser parked at the turnoff to the sting site. Inside was one of Tuttle's top people, a guy named Pettigrew."

Ethan nodded. "I know him."

"He had a legitimate message for Tuttle, but there was no reason for him to be out there in a marked car. Except to warn away Skid."

"Has he confessed?" Ethan asked.

Zoe looked to Whitby, who nodded. "He's making a deal."

Continuing, Zoe said, "I walked in on a meeting Prescott had with the FBI agent in charge of the shooting investigation. He'd called Chickie in, too, to hear his suspicions about Feller County police involvement in the drug bust. There are plenty of people who can testify to his escalating fear.

"Out at Fitzgerald's house, Farmer and Prescott were waiting. Farmer was expecting a deal, and Prescott was hoping Skid would show up, even though it was the wrong place. Skid had gotten the directions Prescott sent him via Farmer. If he showed up, it would mean he could trust Feller County police. If Skid didn't show, Prescott knew he was in trouble."

"All the time they waited for Skid." Whitby said, "Farmer kept bragging about the inside connection. Farmer claims he was nervous, and that's why he kept talking, but maybe he could see the effect it was having on Prescott.

"While they waited, Prescott showed Farmer his weapon, and they did a little target practice before deciding they might disturb unseen neighbors. Prescott had the gun outfitted with a shell catcher, and he was explaining the advantages of using one when you happened to pull up the drive."

There was a catch in Zoe's voice as she said, "Prescott thought you were Tuttle. He saw the word 'Sheriff' on your door, and all he could think was that Tuttle had finally dropped his stupid act and come after him. He saw the figure in the passenger seat and figured that was Skid. He says he started shooting before he even realized his finger was on the trigger."

Whitby slid his hand under Ethan's, palm to palm, hooking thumbs with him and squeezing. "With everyone singing—Pettigrew, Farmer, Prescott himself—I don't think we'll have any problems with conviction. Attempted murder, as well as murder."

Zoe added a nod to punctuate Whitby's statement.

Ethan's brows drew together. "It's too bad, though. He was a good cop." Then added, "How about Ren?"

"The hero of our story," Whitby smiled. "Zoe suggested she might do well in peer counseling."

Zoe nodded again. "Whitby's the one who found a good place. It's part of the same overall organization as the rehab facility where you'll be going. Ren's mother hasn't given the final okay to it yet. I think she's afraid she'll have to admit there are problems in the family, but she knows she has to face her own lies. Her nephew,

Ellis Anton, has been arrested. From what I understand, truck-loads of photos are being hauled out of his studio. And he's got a web site, too. Well, he *had* one.

"Up until now, Ren thought she was the only one—that it really was something terrible in her that made her cousin treat her as he did." Zoe shivered with distaste. "Here's hoping he gets locked up for a good long time."

Closing his eyes, Ethan nodded. "Always did wonder about Ren," he said in a half-whisper. Blinking heavily before his eyelids drifted shut again, he added, "Still, I'm not going to miss her stories."

And a slight smile settled on his lips as sleep overtook him.

Other Mysteries Available from Spinsters Ink

Booked for Murder, Val McDermid. $12.00

Closed in Silence, Joan M. Drury. $10.95

Common Murder, Val McDermid. $10.95

Conferences Are Murder, Val McDermid. $12.00

Deadline for Murder, Val McDermid. $10.95

The Hangdog Hustle, Elizabeth Pincus. $9.95

The Lessons, Melanie McAllester. $9.95

The Other Side of Silence, Joan M. Drury. $9.95

Ordinary Justice, Trudy Labovitz $12.00

Report for Murder, Val McDermid. $10.95

Silent Words, Joan M. Drury. $10.95

The Solitary Twist, Elizabeth Pincus $9.95

The Two-Bit Tango, Elizabeth Pincus. $9.95

The Well-Heeled Murders, Cherry Hartman $10.95

Spinsters Ink was founded in 1978 to produce books for diverse women's communities. In 1986, we merged with Aunt Lute Books to become Spinsters/Aunt Lute. In 1990, the Aunt Lute Foundation became an independent nonprofit publishing program. In 1992, Spinsters moved to Minnesota.

Spinsters Ink publishes novels and nonfiction works that deal with significant issues in women's lives from a feminist perspective: books that not only name these crucial issues, but—more important—encourage change and growth. We are committed to publishing works by women writing from the periphery: fat women, Jewish women, lesbians, old women, poor women, rural women, women examining classism, women of color, women with disabilities, women who are writing books that help make the best in our lives more possible.

Spinsters titles are available from your local bookseller or by mail order through Spinsters Ink. A free catalog is available upon request. Please include $2.00 shipping for the first title ordered and 50¢ for every title thereafter. Visa and Mastercard are accepted.

Spinsters Ink
32 E. First St., #330
Duluth, MN 55802-2002
USA

(phone) 218-727-3222   (fax) 218-727-3119
(e-mail) spinster@spinsters-ink.com
(website) http://www.spinsters-ink.com

Deadly Embrace is Trudy Labovitz's second book in the Zoe Kergulin series. The first was *Ordinary Justice*.